**She stared a**  **,**
**checked the**  **s**
**to make sure she was reading it**
**properly, checked the line again,**
**then gave a whoop of joy.**

She *was* pregnant! It had happened!

She couldn't stop smiling. To have a baby—
to have a child on whom she could lavish a
mother's love—the love she'd missed out on
as a child. Yes, her father had been wonderful,
but she knew instinctively a mother's love was
different.

Theo!

How could she be so excited when she felt, deep
in her heart, Theo really didn't want another
child?

Although now they knew each other better,
might things not work out?

Might she not be able to have Theo *and* a child?

But the excitement she'd felt when she first saw
the confirmation failed to return. She might
have fallen in love with Theo, but in no way had
he indicated he had similar feelings for her...

At least she'd have his child...

# JIMMIE'S CHILDREN'S UNIT

*The Children's Cardiac Unit,*
*St James's Hospital, Sydney.*
*A specialist unit where the dedicated staff*
*mend children's hearts...and their own!*

# THE HEART SURGEON'S BABY SURPRISE

BY
MEREDITH WEBBER

⊚™ MILLS & BOON®
*Pure reading pleasure*™

All the characters in this book have no existence outside the imagination of the author, and have no relation whatsoever to anyone bearing the same name or names. They are not even distantly inspired by any individual known or unknown to the author, and all the incidents are pure invention.

First published in Great Britain 2008
Paperback edition 2009
Harlequin Mills & Boon Limited,
Eton House, 18-24 Paradise Road, Richmond, Surrey TW9 1SR

© Meredith Webber 2008

ISBN: 978 0 263 86824 1

Set in Times Roman 10½ on 12 pt
03-0209-45411

Printed and bound in Spain
by Litografia Rosés, S.A., Barcelona

**Meredith Webber** says of herself, 'Some ten years ago, I read an article which suggested that Mills and Boon were looking for new medical authors. I had one of those "I can do that" moments, and gave it a try. What began as a challenge has become an obsession—though I do temper the "butt on seat" career of writing with dirty but healthy outdoor pursuits, fossicking through the Australian Outback in search of gold or opals. Having had some success in all of these endeavours, I now consider I've found the perfect lifestyle.'

**Recent titles by the same author:**

THE HEART SURGEON'S SECRET CHILD**
CHILDREN'S DOCTOR, MEANT-TO-BE WIFE†
THE SHEIKH SURGEON'S BABY*
DESERT DOCTOR, SECRET SHEIKH*
A PREGNANT NURSE'S CHRISTMAS WISH
THE NURSE HE'S BEEN WAITING FOR†

**Jimmie's Children's Unit
*Desert Doctors
†Crocodile Creek

# CHAPTER ONE

SHE was tall, she was blonde and she was beautiful. Theo Corones watched from the back of the team meeting as all the men in the room, most of whom were married, registered this fact.

'Grace Sutherland, paediatric cardiac surgeon, trained in Cape Town, South Africa, then further studies in the UK. My main area of expertise is paediatric heart transplants.'

'Of course, you're a South African and following in famous footsteps,' Alex Attwood, the head of the paediatric cardiac surgery team at St James's Children's Hospital, teased gently.

Was it because he was still thinking how beautiful she was that Theo saw the puzzled look on her face? She was intelligent enough to know from his voice that Alex was teasing her, so it seemed she wasn't used to being teased.

Theo thought back to the briefing notes he'd had on the two new surgeons. Jean-Luc Fournier was from France, thirty-four years old and already considered good enough to head up a new unit at a hospital in Marseilles, and Grace Sutherland, thirty-five...

Surely by thirty-five you'd got used to being teased.

The meeting proceeded and Theo turned his attention to it, but that expression on Grace Sutherland's face was like a missed note in a piece of music, so it stuck in a corner of his mind.

'Grace, you'll be working on Phil's team, while Jean-Luc will work on mine. This is only for the first three months, then you'll swap over so you both have a chance to see the two of us at work. Not that you'll be observers—no, you'll be operating with us and, when we're not available, for us. And for that reason it's important you know the whole team. Maggie Park, Phil's wife, usually works as my anaesthetist—take a bow, Mags—while Aaron Gilchrist is the anaesthetist on Phil's team.'

Aaron waved his hand at the two newcomers, while Alex went on to introduce the other theatre staff, nurses, registrars and residents who worked with the team.

'And so we come to Theo, who works on both teams. At the moment we only have the one bypass machine—well, we have three but two are being modified to different specifications. Theo is working with the engineers in what spare time he gets—so he works with whoever is doing a procedure that requires bypass.'

Theo nodded his acknowledgement of the introduction but as both newcomers turned towards him he saw Grace Sutherland's eyes for the first time. A pale clear blue, like the aquamarine stone in a ring his mother wore—like morning sky after a night of rain had cleared the dust and smog from the city...

'Theo!'

Alex's voice wasn't exactly sharp but it made it clear Theo had missed some part of the conversation.

'Sorry, Alex, you were saying?'

'I was telling Grace and Jean-Luc you also ran the ECMO machines and would walk them through the way we use both machines later today.'

'I'd be glad to,' Theo replied, annoyed with himself for missing this conversation the first time. He was *always* focussed on work. And to be distracted by a blonde with aquamarine eyes—impossible!

Grace studied the man who worked the bypass machines. She'd been intrigued by his background when she'd read the notes she'd been given—brief bios of all members of the team.

What was different about Theo was that while most perfusionists—people specially trained to run bypass and extracorporeal membrane oxygenation machines—were from a nursing background, Theo had been—and still was, she assumed—a doctor. A surgeon, in fact, who, for reasons unmentioned in the bio had turned from operating on small children to running the machines that kept them alive, before, after and during delicate operations.

It was a puzzle and she didn't like puzzles. She'd have to ask him about it.

And now she'd sorted that out, she should stop looking at him—looking at him wasn't going to provide an answer. But looking at him had made her register that he was a particularly good-looking man, big without being bulky, black hair shot through with silver here and there, dark eyes below well-shaped eyebrows. Her father always kept his eyebrows tidy, bemoaning the fact that many men, as they aged, didn't bother.

It was, she realised, even as she considered Theo Corones's eyebrows, a totally absurd thing for her to be thinking about in a team meeting and, sadly, a reflection of just how unlike other women she was! Other women, she was sure, would be checking out the straight nose and the full, well-defined lips and the way his profile resembled that of old Greek statues, but not her—she'd picked on eyebrows as a feature in his favour.

She sighed, aware she was so unlike other women she needed a planet of her own. Men were from Mars, women from Venus, and Grace from a galaxy far, far away…

The meeting broke up, and Jean-Luc, who would be living in the flat beneath hers for the six months she would be working in Sydney, was chatting to Maggie Park. That was another thing about people from galaxies far, far away—they couldn't chat.

'Would you like to see the machines now?'

She was pondering her inability to chat and assuring herself, for perhaps the millionth time, that it didn't matter, when Theo asked the question. He'd come from somewhere behind her so she'd had no warning of his approach, and, being unprepared, his deep, velvety voice had sparked a peculiar reaction in her skin—prickly, like mild sunburn making its presence felt at the end of a day at the beach.

'I could come now but Jean-Luc looks as if he's busy,' she replied, checking out Theo's eyebrows close up and confirming they really were wonderful—strong, but neat, and with a decided arch.

'Then I will show you first and Jean-Luc some other

time,' Theo said calmly, putting out his hand as if to usher her ahead of him.

'Isn't that a nuisance for you?'

Grace had no idea why she was feeling unsettled, but she was—and even more unsettled when he added, 'It will be my pleasure.'

He didn't mean it in any other way than that he loved showing off his machines and twice was better than once, while his tone of voice suggested nothing more than cool politeness. She knew that, but the prickly sunburn effect continued as she left the room with him.

'Why the switch from surgery to perfusionist?' she asked as they entered the lift to go down a floor to see the infants on ECMO.

He looked at her for a moment, then smiled, his teeth very white against his olive skin.

'Straight to the point,' he said. 'Are you always so blunt?'

Grace pretended to consider this—for all of two seconds—before replying.

'I hope people don't think of me as blunt but, yes, I do find asking questions is the easiest way to get answers.'

Theo ushered her out of the lift, nodding as he went.

'Cuts out a lot of chit-chat,' he agreed. 'What's the next question?'

'Why aren't you married?'

Oops! That surprised even her, although undoubtedly her subconscious mind had sorted through the list of staff, checked the bios and, like a good computer, come up with four possible candidates for her Grand Plan—which probably should be labelled Grace's

Silliest Idea Yet. Theo was one of these, Jean-Luc another. Living in the flat above his, she'd have ample time to check out Jean-Luc, but she wasn't sure how often she'd come into contact with Theo.

Hence the question…

Not that he'd answered either of her questions, parrying the first with one of his own and ignoring the second! She hoped it was because they'd walked into the paediatric intensive care unit, not because he was so insulted he'd never speak to her again. She found it difficult enough to make friends—to trust people enough to let them into her life—without setting colleagues against her from the first meeting.

'This is Scarlett Robinson. She was born with hypoplastic left heart syndrome and although Phil and Alex at first decided to do the first-stage operation, she hasn't been well enough and now they're considering heart transplantation if we can get hold of a donor heart.'

'Without doing even the first-stage op—a Norwood to connect the right ventricle to the aorta?' Grace asked, looking down at the tiny baby girl and wondering, as she always did, why some embryonic hearts formed perfectly while others, like Scarlett's, had a very under-developed left side.

'She's not tolerating drugs particularly well,' Theo explained, 'and after a lot of thought and consultation her parents, who live way out west in the bush, decided that rather than weaken her further with the first of the three HLHS ops, we'd list her for a transplant.'

Grace stared at the little girl, all alone in the hospital, and though she told herself Scarlett didn't know she was all alone, and in fact she wasn't, surrounded as she was by staff, Grace still felt a flutter in the region of her heart which could only be sympathy for the baby.

But the one thing she'd learned very early on in her medical career was never to show what she was feeling—especially not when babies were concerned. It was her job to be detached because, as numerous lecturers and professors and even her own father had told her, she could be more help to the patient that way.

So in case Theo had caught a glimpse of her momentary weakness, she spoke with cool, calm competence as she pointed out the downside of this.

'And in the meantime, she's on ECMO which could have devastating consequences on her other organs if she's on it for too long.'

Theo turned to her and shook his head.

'You certainly believe in telling it like it is,' he said, but Grace thought she detected a smile behind the words. 'You're right, of course, but it was up to her parents to make the decision and now my job is to keep her alive on the least amount of support she can handle. Because of her condition she has to be on full support, so the machine is helping both her lungs and her malformed heart do their jobs, but by gearing it down as much as possible I'm hoping to avoid things like brain haemorrhages or kidney problems.'

'Hard to get a heart small enough for her,' Grace murmured, her eyes feasting on the tiny infant, thinking of other newborns she'd operated on—thinking of other infants.

Or one other infant...

One hypothetical infant...

Could she *do* it? Could she ask some man…?

'But they do come up,' Theo said, and Grace stared at him, struggling against the thoughts that kept intruding, thoughts she knew were stupid and sentimental and all the things she didn't want to be—thoughts about a baby of her own…

She pulled herself together, hiding the moment of weakness behind a bland observation.

'It's usually women who are unrealistically optimistic,' she said.

Theo frowned.

'I don't consider optimism a gender-based trait, and pointing out that small hearts do become available was stating a fact, not being unrealistic.'

As the words came out he realised he was being as blunt as his colleague—was it catching, this brusqueness of hers?

And as for the question he hadn't answered earlier, what business was it of hers why he wasn't married?

Ah! He'd answered his own question. He probably wasn't getting as snappy as Grace Sutherland, but she'd prodded a sore spot he rarely thought about these days, and *his* brusqueness was reaction to her prodding.

'Where are her parents?'

Another question but at least one he could answer.

'Her mother was here. She flew down with the Royal Flying Doctor Service when they brought the baby to us. But she had to go home to the rest of the family—she's hoping to get down again next week but even with really cheap accommodation available at the hospital, she still has to pay air fares and, I imagine, pay someone to mind the other children at home.'

'Poor thing, it must be so hard to not be able to be with her baby,' Grace murmured, but in such a way Theo had to look at her. Did she really feel for Scarlett's mother or was she mouthing a platitude while thinking something else entirely?

He didn't know this woman so he had no idea and, really, did it matter? Yet again he sensed a puzzle…

They'd moved away from Scarlett's crib, out of the PICU to the lift foyer where they met up with other members of the team waiting to go down.

'Grace and I are barely settled in and, speaking for myself, I need to shop before I can eat,' Jean-Luc said, joining his and Grace's names in a way that suggested a relationship, although as far as Theo knew they'd only met since their separate arrivals in Australia. 'Is there a good restaurant close by?'

'Scoozi!'

Jean-Luc had spoken to Aaron who was standing beside him, but the reply was chorused by most of the team.

'It's the other side of the park,' Jasmine Summers, one of the PICU nurses added as they all stepped into the lift. 'Some of us are going there now, so do come along. You're coming, aren't you, Theo?'

He *had* intended going home to do some work on a wood-fired oven he was building in his tiny courtyard, but he had to eat.

And Grace Sutherland, for all her blunt questions, intrigued him…

'Oh, do come, Theo.' Now she added her entreaty, and though he had the strangest—and strongest—feeling he was being manipulated, he agreed.

Out of curiosity, he told himself, and in part that was the truth, because there was something about Grace Sutherland that didn't quite ring true—some mystery inside the beautiful packaging.

That she was physically attractive to him was a secondary matter, or so he assured himself. He didn't get involved with work colleagues so the physical attraction would never be explored, but the intrigue? It wouldn't hurt to investigate that, surely...

The group walked in a straggle of twos and threes down the road that ran alongside the park towards the restaurant. Grace walked in the lead with Phil, Theo behind them with Maggie and Aaron, and though he was listening to the conversation about titration rates of drugs during open-heart surgery in very small infants, he wasn't taking in as much of it as he usually did.

She walked with a peculiar grace—what a stupid thing to be thinking about a woman called Grace!—but the way she strode along, her pace matching Phil's suggested an athleticism that wasn't often seen in specialists of either gender, most of whom were too busy to get to the gym with any regularity or to work out in other ways.

The staff at Scoozi, seeing the mob from the hospital arrive, pushed together a number of tables, but was it chance that Grace sat next to Theo, who had taken the chair at one end?

'You didn't answer my question,' she said, answering his own query—the seating arrangement had *not* been chance.

'Question?' he parried, although he knew full well what she'd asked. But now, rather than consider the woman's grace, he was considering her lack of it. And her lack of good manners! It was none of her business why he'd switched from surgery to perfusion.

'Why aren't you married?'

He'd forgotten that one! He stared at her, aware his disbelief was probably written on his face. It must have been for she looked embarrassed, but only for a moment, recovering her composure beautifully and smiling an apology.

'I know that's personal, but I'm only here for six months and if I want to get to know everyone in the team, then I have to ask questions.'

That kind of made sense—or did it?

'Do you *really* want to get to know everyone in the team? After all, as you say, you're only here six months, after which you'll go back to South Africa, send emails for a few months, Christmas cards for a few years, then forget the lot of us.'

'Probably not Christmas cards, I'm not good with them.' She looked embarrassed, as if he'd been spot on in the reading of her character. Not that she was going to let him get away with it. She shifted slightly in her chair then continued, 'But professionally it's good to keep in touch with people, especially those with more experience, because you never know when something comes up you haven't personally experienced before, and you can always ask.'

She hadn't answered *his* question, but her comments made him wonder even more about this woman. In his life, women were the ones who kept the strands of friendship sewn together, his mother and aunts keeping in touch with the family's friends, while his ex-wife had been forever on the net, talking to one friend or another, and had turned the sending out of Christmas cards into a kind of 'who gets the most' contest. But, then, Lena was like that...

'You're thinking about some woman now,' the exasperating South African said, her clipped accent seeming to turn the remark into a rebuke.

'You can't know that!' Theo growled. 'And if there's one thing I hate, it's someone—usually a woman—telling me what I'm thinking.'

'Well, you were scowling,' Grace replied, totally unabashed. 'The kind of scowl that suggests bad thoughts, and as you're hardly likely to be thinking bad thoughts about your bypass machine, or the menu that's in your hands, I guessed it must have had something to do with my question.'

He scowled some more and began to read the menu, although he knew it by heart and always ordered the Creole pizza and out of sheer politeness should have passed it to Grace, had she not annoyed him so much.

'I'll have the Creole pizza,' she announced, Jasmine, on her other side, having handed her a menu. 'Chicken, banana, sweet chilli sauce and sour cream—Italian purists must be turning over in their graves but it sounds delicious.'

*Now* what was he going to order? If he ordered the Creole she'd think he was copying her and probably read something into it—like he might be interested in her.

Which he was in the way a scientist was interested in a new specimen that appeared under his microscope, but no more than that, for all the unexpected tugs of attraction he was feeling.

Heaven forbid!

He ordered a steak and a glass of the pinot grigio the restaurateur, Anna, imported from Italy. Someone further down the table had ordered a plate of garlic bread and another of brushetta before anyone was seated, and these arrived as the orders were taken, the plates of bread being passed around.

'No, thank you,' Grace said to both.

'Dieting?' Jasmine asked, and Theo watched, wondering just how Grace would respond.

'No, I never diet,' she said, with the supreme confidence of a woman with a great metabolism.

End of conversation, although Jasmine had obviously meant it as an opening gambit.

'Lucky you,' Jasmine told her, not willing to let the subject go just yet. 'I'm always dieting. I've tried just about every diet ever written.'

'Oh, but surely you don't need to diet, Jasmine.'

Other women might have said the same reassuring words without Theo even noticing, but to him it sounded as if Grace was making an effort to be nice—as if social chatter didn't come easily to her.

Jasmine, too, must have sensed something strange for she smiled uncertainly, conveying enough apprehension for even someone as seemingly insensitive as Grace to see.

'I didn't mean to sound critical of diets or people who diet,' she added quickly. 'But research has shown that dieting fads can do more harm than good.'

For Theo it was like watching an act in a play and he waited to see if Jasmine would be mollified.

Apparently she was, for she smiled at Grace.

'I know,' she said with a big sigh. 'I've read that too, but I think I'm addicted to diets.'

It was said as a joke, but, sensing it would go straight over Grace's head, Theo plunged in.

'Like I'm addicted to good pizza,' he said, forgetting he'd just ordered steak. 'Which is why I'm spending all my off-duty time building a wood-fired oven in my already too small courtyard.'

'Is the pizza no good here that you didn't order it?'

Of course Grace had picked up on his error.

'No, the pizzas are great, I just needed a change,' he assured her. OK, so she'd zeroed in on him again, but at least discussing food likes and dislikes was better than discussing marriage—or his lack thereof. And Jasmine was off the hook—she'd turned to talk to Aaron on her other side, so Theo took another slice of garlic bread and relaxed.

'So, are you in a relationship?'

Had he heard correctly? He stared at the woman he thought had asked an extremely impertinent question and she gave an embarrassed shrug.

'I told you I asked questions—I explained why,' she said. 'And you didn't answer about why you're not married, so I wondered...'

Theo studied her a moment longer, sensing something he couldn't quite pin down behind the brash manner.

Something uncertain?

It sounded that way, but surely not!

Given the attraction he felt towards her, he knew he had to keep his distance, not find excuses to learn more of her.

'Why?' he asked, cool and distant again. 'Why are you wondering—why do you need to know? As you said, you're here for six months. I could work with people for six months and not need to know about their personal lives. In fact, there are people at this table— No, that's not right, the team mostly know the surface things about each other's lives, although the fact that I am single is enough for most of them to know. No one in the eight months I've been here has ever asked me why.'

'Yes, well…'

She pursed her lips—lush, full lips which, when pursed, looked extremely inviting and turned the tug into a more insistent feeling—and studied him in turn, then shook her head.

'I'm sorry! I've been far too intrusive. My father was always telling me that, right from when I was a small girl, asking questions all the time and not differentiating between acceptable questions and personal ones. Although—'

She stopped, and Theo forgot he was trying to keep his distance and was intrigued enough to prompt her.

'Although?' he echoed, and she smiled and shook her head, the blue eyes looking…sad? Vulnerable?

Vulnerable? This super-confident woman?

Super-efficient, too, he suspected.

Vulnerable was the last word he'd use…

She'd gone too far. Again! Grace knew that, but somehow the switch that turned her off before she pushed that extra bit further had always been missing from her genetic programming. She should never have asked him about his marital state in the first place, then pushing when he didn't answer…

Terrible!

But he'd be ideal. She'd known that from the moment she'd seen him, recalling his bio in the team info sheets she'd read. He was intelligent, well-built, good-looking— although she knew that shouldn't be a prerequisite—and apparently available. Not that she needed available—she wasn't intending to have an affair with him.

All she really wanted was his sperm...

She felt a blush stealing into her cheeks and was furious with herself. She might be blessed with a good metabolism so didn't need to diet, but she'd have preferred a tendency to run to fat than this terrible blushing thing she had.

Had Theo seen the colour in her cheeks that he lifted the bottle of cold water off the table and offered to pour her a glass? How embarrassing!

Surely this was the time to ditch the Grand Plan— to forget all about it and just get on with her life. She'd lived with the ache for a long time—she could live with it a little longer...

She thanked him and watched his concentration as he poured the water, then noticed the back of his hand as he passed her the glass—long slim fingers and a slight scattering of dark hair at the wrist—and for some strange reason the heat of embarrassment left her, and a shiver travelled up her spine.

Looking at a man's hand couldn't make you shiver, so maybe she was sickening for something.

Not that she ever got sick...

'Although?' he said again, and it took her a couple of seconds to go back far enough to pick up the prompt.

She smiled. Father had told her when she was very young that she had a beautiful smile and that you could never go wrong with a smile.

'I can't tell you the "although",' she said, wondering if this was flirting. 'But I *am* interested.'

Duh! Blushing again. Who would have thought it would be this hard?

'In me?' Theo asked, and she felt her blush deepen so she must be scarlet-cheeked by now.

'In everyone on the team,' she said.

'Oh!' His dark brown eyes lit up to match his delighted smile. 'So you'll ask all of them about their relationships? Actually, I can fill you in on some of them. Jasmine's just got engaged, Phil and Alex and Aaron—with Aldo added we have a lot of *A*s, don't we? Anyway those three are all happily married—'

'Stop! You're making me more and more embarrassed. It *is* none of my business.'

Theo stopped, but only because she sounded genuinely distressed, although he was pretty sure Dr Grace Sutherland didn't often do distressed. But it was there again, that note of uncertainty in a person who gave off such positive vibes, and he was interested in spite of himself.

In a purely professional way, of course.

'I'm not in a relationship,' he said, under the cover of the noise as meals were delivered to the table. 'And I *was* married, but my wife and I split up seven years ago.'

Wrong thing to tell her. That interested look was back in her eyes.

'Do you know the number of weeks, days and hours

as well?' she asked, spearing a shard of red-hot pain dead-centre into his heart.

'As a matter of fact, I do,' he said, his voice as cold and as curt as he could make it. His meal was placed in front of him and he looked at it and shook his head, aware he'd never eat it, although, thinking now of Elena, he wouldn't have eaten the pizza either.

He didn't look at Grace again in case he was inveigled into thinking her vulnerable again. Vulnerable as a full-grown crocodile! So he cut his steak, and pretended to eat, shifting things around on his plate so it looked as if some of the food had disappeared.

'I know that trick,' his colleague said, leaning a little closer so she could speak quietly, a drift of a very feminine perfume—orange blossom?—assailing his nostrils. 'I've done it myself many a time. I'm sorry if I upset you, asking about your wife. I didn't mean to. It was just the way you said seven years—it sounded as if you'd been counting. That means it must have hurt.'

He'd been determined to ignore her, but from the very formal way she spoke he guessed apologising was rare for her, and one look into the crystalline blue eyes confirmed that she was upset.

And so was he, but for more dubious reasons! Those eyes held the same fascination as her pursed lips had earlier and he definitely didn't do relationships with colleagues.

Although she was only here for six months—

No! He had to stop this!

Now!

'We had a car accident, our daughter died, my wife

blamed me, but it is my daughter's death that's imprinted on my mind, not my wife leaving me.'

Grace reared back in her seat, feeling as winded as if he'd struck her with his hand.

How *did* she get herself into these situations?

Because she had a one-track mind, that's how!

Why *couldn't* she do normal chit-chat, like other women?

Theo had pushed his plate away and was standing up, and much as she'd have liked to stand up with him, to follow him wherever he was going so she could apologise, she knew he'd revealed his pain to a virtual stranger for one reason and one reason only—to repel her.

She watched him, aware everyone at the table must be wondering what the South African woman had done to upset him.

'Eat your pizza, act normal—that's if you know how to!' he muttered to her as he bent to push his chair back into place. Then he straightened and faced the rest of the gathering. 'Sorry, folks, not feeling the best.'

He walked away, stopping to talk to the waitress who'd served them, money changing hands.

'He must have been feeling a bit off all along,' Jasmine said. 'Ordering steak when he always orders the Creole pizza.'

Grace looked at the pizza growing colder on her plate and understood why he hadn't ordered it. But he'd been right, she had to eat some of it because not eating it would look suspicious. She picked up a slice and bit into it, recognising that the mix of flavours was indeed delicious, although the food seemed to be turning to sawdust in her mouth.

A car accident—losing a daughter. The poor man! And for all he was so perfect, she'd have to cross him off the list.

Although…

She thought it through, looking at the idea from all angles, finally coming to the conclusion that maybe what she was offering was just what Theo needed.

In the back of her head she heard her father warning her that her solutions might not always be what was best for other people, but that had been when she'd been dealing with some of the poor families at home, ruthlessly reorganising their lives into some semblance of order.

This was different.

A child that was yet wasn't his.

No responsibility.

No need to get emotionally involved.

With either her or the child…

Yes, it could work.

'Does he live somewhere nearby?' she heard herself ask Jasmine, then, in case the question was too obvious, she added, 'Perhaps someone should call in and see if he's OK.'

Jasmine looked at her, then smiled.

'He's OK and even if he wasn't, he wouldn't want anyone fussing over him,' she said. 'He's a very private man, our Theo. I'd better tell you that he never gets involved with colleagues. Believe me, many have tried but none have succeeded. It's kind of like a golden rule with him.'

Well, really! Grace thought, annoyed with Jasmine for assuming—quite correctly—that she was interested in Theo, and horrified with herself for being so obvious about it.

'It's a good rule,' she managed, realising some response was necessary. 'Relationships at work can get very messy.'

'Or can work brilliantly,' Jasmine said, nodding towards Maggie and Phil, who were laughing together at the far end of the table. 'We had three couples fall in love within the unit only last year, so don't think you'll be immune to love while you're here in Oz.'

She paused and studied Grace for a moment.

'Unless, of course, there's a very special man back home in South Africa?' she teased.

Grace thought of the very special man back home and smiled.

'Oh, yes, there is,' she said, but she didn't add that it was because of him—well, partly because of him—that she was interested in Theo. Someone like Jasmine, recently engaged to the man she loved, would never understand Grace's plan or the means by which she hoped to implement it...

# CHAPTER TWO

THEO watched as Grace attached the PVC tube from the bypass machine to the cannula inserted into the right side of little Adelaide Matthews's heart. She worked quickly but carefully, her movements so precise and economical he had to admire them.

With the ingoing tube attached to the cannula already inserted into the aorta, she stepped back to let Phil get closer.

'On pump,' Phil said, the order crisp and quiet, and Theo started the machine, watching closely to see that the heparin given to thin the blood had been sufficient to prevent clotting, watching the pressure—Adelaide was three and needed more pressure than a baby but less than a five-year-old—watching for anything to go wrong.

'Plege on.' Now Phil fed the cardioplegia—a potassium poison—into the heart to stop it beating. When it worked, in a matter of minutes, he could begin.

The operation, to correct a problem with the coronary arteries which had been repositioned during an earlier operation for transposition of the great arteries, shouldn't have been difficult, but scans had shown that one of the coronary arteries had grown through the wall of the heart, like a hose going in through the side of a bucket then back out again, and needed total repositioning.

Aware it could take some time, Theo was overly conscious of his patient's status, checking the monitors constantly, noting the various pressures, the ECG, co-agulation values, blood gases and electrolytes. But mainly it was controlling the pump that absorbed him. Too little blood flow and the patient could suffer oxygen deprivation to her brain, too much and it could blow her delicate little blood vessels apart.

Why did a surgeon turn to this job? Grace had asked, but the satisfaction he found in getting a patient through an often long and complex operation in as good a condition as possible, was a source of enormous satisfaction, and already some of his refinements to the bypass machine were being used worldwide.

Why not?

He looked across at Grace—well, at the hooded, gowned, bespectacled figure he knew was Grace—and was sorry he hadn't answered that particular question.

Wouldn't have an opportunity now, having spoken so abruptly to her the previous evening…

'Theo?'

Knowing what Phil was asking, he recited all the information he had to hand, adding that Adelaide was doing very well.

'So why change from surgery?'

Three operations later, he'd just emerged from the shower in the theatre changing rooms, a towel wrapped around his waist, when Grace, in bra and panties—her figure was superb—asked the question he'd decided she would never ask again.

He stared at her, debating whether to answer, but as everyone else was gone—he always stayed back to ensure personally that the machine was properly sterilised and sealed—there was really no reason why he shouldn't tell her.

Particularly as she was pulling on a crisp white shirt, buttoning it up, drawing his attention to her breasts in a way that was totally out of order—he changed with women all the time and *never* looked at their breasts!

'I injured my hands—for a while I couldn't operate—but the world of paediatric cardiac surgery had been my focus as I trained, through basic surgery, then cardiac surgery. I'd finally made it as a registrar on the paeds cardiac team and I didn't want to leave it. Probably out of pity, my old boss, the chief surgeon at the hospital, suggested I have a go at perfusion while my hands healed. I did a course, learned even more from the woman who had run the machine for our team, then began to see possibilities of improving the system, which was when I became hooked. To me, keeping a child as stable as possible while on pump—and even more importantly while on ECMO—has become my obsession.'

'So much so you never considered going back to operating?'

He paused, looking at his hands.

'My hands were burnt, the tendons damaged, and although they healed, it worried me that they had probably lost some sensitivity.'

He paused, remembering the pain of those years—
so much pain, the least of it physical.

'I wondered if I would still have the feel you need
to put a stitch the size of a pinhead into a vein with the
diameter of a hair. I decided I couldn't take the risk.'

'That's an incredibly honest answer,' she said, looking puzzled again.

'Did you think I'd lie?' he demanded angrily, his
emotions already stirred up with memories. And on top
of that, it was the puzzled look he caught on her face that
gave the impression of vulnerability despite suspecting
she was about as vulnerable as a slab of concrete.

Although more shapely…

She grinned at him, totally disarming him.

'No, I suppose not, but it's the kind of thing I might
have said and I'm forever being told I should pretty
things up more. Too blunt, too abrasive, too intrusive—
I'm all those "toos"!'

'You are too,' he said, suddenly liking her, for all the
intrusiveness and abrasion. Although she didn't smile
at his feeble joke and he wondered if he could really
like someone with no sense of humour.

Grace knew she should have smiled, but it was a
feeble attempt at a joke and she had just put him back
onto her list of possibles again. In fact, it was hardly a
list—his being the only name on it.

'And being blunt and abrasive…' she said, deciding
it was better to get things out into the open as soon as
possible. That way she'd know where she stood. 'I wondered if I could ask you something.'

'You didn't ask if you could ask before asking me
all kinds of personal questions yesterday,' he reminded

her, leaning back against the doorjamb in a way that made all the muscles of his chest stand out so all of a sudden he was an extremely sexy man as well as a colleague.

Sexy man? *What* was she thinking?

She forced her mind back to her problem.

'Well, this is really very personal to me and very private so I have to believe that if I ask, you won't repeat it.'

He didn't answer, which she took for assent, but the words she needed were jammed in her throat.

Not easy words to say in any circumstances and she'd got off on the wrong foot with this man…

Make amends first?

'Are you finished for the day? I feel after last night I owe you a meal. I ruined your dinner, firstly by ordering your favourite pizza, although you *could* still have ordered it, then by asking intrusive questions. Could we go there again—or somewhere else—and I'll pay?'

What was with this woman? Theo watched her as she pulled on a skirt, tucking the shirt she'd put on earlier efficiently into the waistband. Even the way she dressed said a lot about her—neat, classy in an understated way, yet still…prim was the only word! But the questions she'd been asking didn't go with that image any more than the classic but boring clothes could successfully hide her sexy body.

Although if he hadn't seen her nearly naked, might he have been quite so aware of it?

And was it because of the sexy body or because of

the inconsistencies he kept finding in her that he heard himself agreeing to have dinner with her?

'An early dinner—I want to spend some time at the hospital later this evening.'

He wasn't sure why he'd added the stipulation. True, he liked to spend time at the hospital but he often came late at night when the unit was quiet and most of the parents were sleeping as fitfully as their hopes and fears for their child would allow.

'Now?'

He studied Grace. Of course he knew why he'd added the stipulation! He was suspicious of her—and doubly suspicious of her interest in him. Most women, even in these enlightened days, were happy to let the men make the running in a developing relationship—and most women were adept at reading the 'not inter-ested' sign he hung around himself at work.

So what was with Grace? Was she so inexperienced—at thirty-five?—that she didn't know the rules, couldn't read the signs? Or did she have some agenda of her own?

Well, yes to the latter, she'd told him as much, but she wasn't giving off 'I'd like to get to know you better' vibes, so what other agenda could it be?

'Of course now, if that suits you,' he said, wonder-ing what he was getting into, suspecting his assumption of her inexperience might be true and intrigued in spite of himself. 'I was always curious.'

She gave him a sharp, assessing look—no fool, this woman—then shrugged.

'I don't mind that,' she assured him. 'In fact, it might be a point in my favour.'

Not smiling so it wasn't a joke—but a point in her favour? In favour of what?

'Shall we continue this mysterious conversation all evening, or should we discuss something else—there's always work—until we've eaten?'

Now she did smile, and although the expression held a degree of uncertainty it confirmed his initial reaction to her—she was beautiful.

But beautiful women usually radiated confidence, and although Grace gave the impression of being in control, and certainly seemed confident in her work, he kept getting the feeling that her personal confidence was something she'd manufactured, like a cloak, that she wrapped around herself to protect the person she really was.

Or was he being fanciful? Seeing something of his own self-protective instincts and habits in her?

They left the hospital and walked down the road, by-passing Scoozi by unspoken but mutual consent and wandering towards a little brasserie, far enough from the hospital to be less populated by medical people.

'Is there pizza on the menu here?' Grace asked, hesitating on the footpath beside the trellised outdoor garden.

'I don't only eat pizza and, in fact, this place does the best moussaka outside my aunt's house in Melbourne.'

Grace glanced at him and he waited, expecting more questions, but none came and he realised that although she was looking at him, her mind was elsewhere.

On the question she wanted to ask?

It was looming larger and larger in his mind, so surely it was swooping around inside her head.

'We're going in?' he asked, and she nodded, though she indicated the outdoor area with a wave of her slim, thin-fingered hand.

'Could we sit outside?'

He was still thinking about her hands—he'd noticed them in Theatre, where, even gloved, they'd looked... aristocratic somehow.

'Of course.'

The waitress seated them at a corner table, close by a rambling vine that drooped tiny purple flowers, dropping them when the wind rustled through the leaves so a vagrant few rested in Grace's golden hair like tiny amethyst gemstones.

Theo opted not to tell her, sure she'd be annoyed by such frivolous beauty and brush them out.

'I'll have the lamb,' Grace announced, one minute's perusal of the menu enough for her to make up her mind. The decisiveness fitted what he knew of her. He ordered moussaka—wondering if she could tell as much about him from his order. A man of habit—that's about all she'd gather.

'So, the question?' he prompted when the waitress had disappeared to the kitchen with their orders.

She seemed startled, then, to his surprise, she blushed.

'It should be easy for a person as blunt and plain-spoken as I am,' she muttered, looking more embarrassed by the second, 'but it's not that kind of question.'

'Oh?'

He wasn't going to help her. He was already regretting agreeing to this dinner. Getting even mildly entangled with a particular member of the team wasn't on his agenda. His private life was just that, private, and he wanted to keep it that way.

'It's personal—very personal—and you'll think I've got a cheek, a terrible cheek. And presumptuous—very presumptuous.'

She stopped and tried a smile that failed dismally, although something about the pathetic attempt struck Theo as brave—valiant.

'Perhaps if I explained, just a little about myself— no, that won't work, it's better just to ask. The thing is, you see, I badly want a child. I'm thirty-five and running out of time, and while I'm here in Sydney is the ideal time to get pregnant and I wondered, if you'd mind—if you had no objections and I know it's a totally outrageous thing to ask, but you're everything that would be fantastic—I wondered if I could use…'

The floundering stopped as suddenly as it had started and, scarlet-faced, she stared at the far corner of the courtyard, swallowing convulsively.

'Don't mind me,' she managed a little later. 'I'm an idiot! Let's just forget all about it and eat.'

'Except our meal hasn't arrived,' he told her, speaking quietly and gently for he could see she was genuinely upset. Somehow she'd convinced herself that whatever it was she wanted to ask was OK, yet when it came to saying it, she'd baulked.

What could have been so outrageous?

He tried to remember what she'd said, but the words, spoken so quickly in her crisp South African voice, had all run together and he'd been more interested in watching her face and seeing her mounting embarrassment to really listen.

'Moussaka?'

'Mine,' he told the waitress, then watched as she placed the lamb dish in front of Grace.

'Perhaps a bottle of wine, the Newnhams Shiraz,' he suggested, more to the waitress than Grace. Neither of them would be involved in Theatre the following day, and the alcohol might help Grace relax.

Though why he was worrying about her, he didn't know. She was a self-confident, thoroughly together woman—and very capable of getting her own way. His presence in this restaurant right now was evidence of that.

Had he ordered the wine to dull the impact of dinner with her? Grace wondered, thinking how idiotic she must have sounded, words somersaulting out of her mouth, tumbling over each other and making no sense at all. She couldn't even remember how far she'd got, her embarrassment so acute her cheeks had been burning!

She tried to concentrate on her meal, which looked and smelled delicious, but she was afraid her hands would shake when she picked up her knife and fork.

'Ah, wine. Try this. It's not well known—in fact, the restaurant gets it from a small producer so you won't find it in bottle shops. You do drink wine?'

Even if she'd been a lifelong and committed teetotaller she'd have agreed to try it. Anything to stop this man thinking she was a complete klutz!

She nodded and watched as he poured the ruby-coloured wine into her glass, then she picked the glass up and lifted it towards him, trying desperately to behave normally, although despair had taken over every cell in her body as she'd finally realised just how stupid her idea had been.

'To your stay in Australia,' he proposed, and Grace acknowledged the toast with a dip of her head. Tiny flowers fell forward onto the table and, realising they must be in her hair, she lifted a hand to brush them out.

'Don't,' he said, reaching out his free hand to catch hers in mid-air. 'They look so pretty.'

'Pretty?' she echoed, the despair finding voice in bitterness. 'That's the last thing anyone's ever called me.'

Still holding her hand, he brought it down to the table, where he rested it, leaving his lying negligently on top of it.

'The flowers are pretty—they're pretty in your hair,' he said, and her bitterness deepened. 'But you, you're way past pretty—you're beautiful.'

He raised his glass again then took a sip of the wine, but she was too flabbergasted by what he'd said to even think about sipping hers.

Beautiful?

He must want something.

She was good-looking, she knew that, even attractive most of the time, but her mouth was too big and her nose too long for beauty and she was too tall…

She shook her head, denying his assertion, and sipped some wine, then wiggled her hand out from under his and tucked it under the table where she had hoped it would stop remembering the feel of the weight of his and the texture of his skin.

Eventually!

'Eat!' he ordered, and by now she was too confused to do anything but obey him.

The meal was delicious, the wine smooth and mellow, slipping down so easily he was filling her glass before she realised she'd emptied it. They talked of the hospital, of the genesis of the paediatric surgery unit at the hospital called Jimmie's, its future, and the people in the team. Doctors and nurses, Theo classified them all for her, every one of them good in their own way but each with special talents.

'And your future—after your time in Sydney?' he asked as the waitress took her plate and she'd said no to dessert. She sat back to enjoy the rest of the wine in her glass, more relaxed than she could believe possible.

'I'll go back home. I've been offered a place on a similar team in Cape Town. My father lives there and as he's not getting any younger I want to be near him.'

'Family's important,' Theo agreed, and whether it was the wine, or that simple statement, or just that she really, really needed to find out if he was the one, she found herself explaining once again.

'My father is to me,' she said. 'He brought me up. My mother died when I was too young to remember her, and though he was a busy man—he was an orthopaedic surgeon—he always had time for me, time to read me a story at bedtime, and to listen to my worries and concerns, and to encourage me to do better, and to help me with my studies.'

She paused, wondering what effect this sudden outpouring of information was having on her companion, but Theo was leaning back in his chair, sipping his wine, if not absorbed in her conversation at least listening politely.

So she barged on, anxious to get it said once and for all.

'It's because of him I want a child—well, partly because of him. He's seventy at the end of the year and I know a grandchild isn't a normal kind of birthday present, but you have to understand my father. He can trace his family back for generations—back to the Scottish Jacobite rebellions, and further, even to the Vikings who conquered parts of Scotland from time to time. His grandfather emigrated to South Africa, but my father has always been interested in his Scottish heritage—in family. But with my mother dying, and him not marrying again, he was left with an only child and one who, at the moment, looks like being the end of the line. I know he's proud of all I've achieved, and he'd never think less of me for not having a child, but deep down I feel I've let him down by not producing one—not producing someone to carry on his bloodline.'

She sneaked another look at Theo but he hadn't fallen asleep neither was he yawning with boredom.

'As I said, I'm thirty-five so I haven't got much time, quite apart from his milestone birthday being this year. Which is what I wanted to ask you—being single and not in a relationship and all. I considered IVF but I don't really want an unknown donor and there'd be no responsibility on your part, of course, it would be like you gave at the sperm bank—'

'Grace!'

He didn't yell her name but he said it with enough force to stop her in mid-flight.

'Yes?'

He'd abandoned his wineglass and his relaxed pose and was leaning forward across the table, frowning fiercely at her.

'Are you for real? Are you honestly sitting there, asking a virtual stranger—we only met yesterday, after all—for some of his sperm? Why not ask some hobo out in the street? For a few dollars you'd probably get all you need. Better still, go down to the beach and ask some of the board-riders—they're outdoors all day, healthy—'

'Stop! What you're saying is ridiculous. Of course, what I asked was ridiculous as well, but you're a doctor, you should understand. If I know where it's come from I have some idea of genetic qualities. Yes, I know it was stupid to ask you when we've only just met, but I've thought about—about getting, you know, into a kind of relationship with someone so I could do this, but I'm not good at flirting and I'm a disaster with relationships, and anyway going to bed with someone I didn't like just to get pregnant seemed wrong somehow, quite apart from the fact that if I did get pregnant I'd feel guilty, as if I'd stolen something from him.'

'And asking a man for some sperm over dinner seemed OK?' His voice, crisp with disbelief, seemed to echo around the outdoor space. She knew she was blushing fiercely again and that made her even angrier—mostly with herself, but surely this man could have been just a little more understanding!

'Of course it's not ideal but when would be? Think about it—halfway through a team meeting can I say, "Would one of you guys mind obliging?" And, anyway, most of the team are married and having a biological child by someone other than their wife, even if they didn't acknowledge it, could cause problems in their marriage. I'm not *totally* insensitive!'

'No?' He was smiling now, the rat! Taking absolute delight in her embarrassment. 'I must say it would enliven team meetings no end for you to suddenly come out with a request for a sperm donor.'

'It's all very well for you to joke,' Grace snapped, hating him more and more for she'd never found it easy to deal with teasing. 'But this is a serious problem for me.'

She sank back in her chair, swigged down the rest of the wine, and sighed.

Theo looked at her, reading the dejection in her pose, the embarrassment that lay behind it, and seeing also, behind the façade of confidence, the motherless little girl who wanted nothing more than to please the father she obviously adored.

It was the little girl who sneaked through his defences, although when he replayed Grace's rationale in his head he suspected there was more to her wanting a child than she'd said. Oh, it had sounded very sensible—but was she using her father's desire to see the family line continued to hide her own longing? He'd seen her at the hospital— seen the way she looked at the small patients—and wondered if she felt it would weaken her somehow to admit she wanted a child for herself?

He sighed.

'Look, I'm sorry for teasing you, and I do see how difficult it must be for you, but if you've thought this through at all, you must realise that the chances of you getting pregnant right off from one…er, donation are very slim. What are you going to do then? Ask someone else?'

She stared at him, such horror in her eyes he knew

immediately she hadn't considered the possibility of *not* getting pregnant straight away.

'But I ovulate regularly and I've been tested and I'm still producing viable eggs so if I time it right, why not? People get pregnant accidentally all the time, so surely if I stick to the right date, so will I.'

Theo shook his head at her desperate protest.

'Are you really such an innocent?' he demanded, then was sorry when he saw the colour creep into her cheeks again. And although he found her blushing attractive he was sure she hated it, so he regretted he'd embarrassed her.

'Of course not!' she said indignantly, but he heard a lie in the words. Then she shrugged her shoulders.

'You must think I'm stupid—stupid for not realizing. Even more stupid for having such a pathetic idea—a baby for a birthday present...'

She stood up, adding, 'Let's go. I'm paying,' in the kind of voice he heard from her in the hospital—cool, efficient, in control.

But not totally in control for her handbag had fallen from her lap, spilling its contents on the floor.

She bent to gather things, obviously flustered, and he bent with her, picking up a lipstick tube, thinking how attractive she was when her mask of self-control slipped. And suddenly the idea of being a sperm donor for this woman didn't seem such a bad idea, although...

'There, I think that's it,' he said, pressing a small pack of tissues into her hand, touching her fingers, looking into her clear eyes, the full lips so close he could have kissed them.

Tension he didn't understand built between them,

growing stronger by the second until he had to diffuse it—or kiss her!

He let her pay the bill, and as they left the restaurant she turned back towards the hospital.

'Aren't you living on Kensington Terrace?' he asked.

She nodded, as if still afraid to speak in case she said something more she'd regret.

'Then you don't have to go back to the hospital. We can walk across the park.'

'Do you live in that direction?' she asked, studying him now, suspicious...

'I don't, I live closer to the city, but it's not much further for me to walk through the park then from your place to the hospital where my car is than it is to walk from here. I'll see you home.'

Definitely suspicious but although her lips—he really had to stop looking at her lips—opened to protest, they closed again, and she didn't shake off his hand when he put it on her elbow to guide her across the road and in through the park gates.

Grace had seen the park in daylight but had not had time to explore it, although someone on the team had mentioned ponds with ducks and geese, and riding trails and dog exercise areas. None of which had much relevance for her, so she'd not taken much notice. And certainly no one had spoken of the romantic possibilities of the area, although as they walked along well-lit paths, in and out of patches of shadows cast by huge old trees, the park assumed a very romantic atmosphere.

Romantic atmosphere? What was wrong with her?

One devastatingly embarrassing meal with a colleague and she was thinking romance?

'Peaceful, isn't it?' Theo remarked, as they wandered along the path through a particularly dense bit of shadow.

'Yes, very!' she said quickly. Peaceful was a *much* better description than romantic!

'You've settled into your flat?' her companion asked, and once again she was grateful. Perhaps he'd forgotten her stupidity at dinner.

'Yes, although I need to find a supermarket and do some proper shopping, and probably find a means of transport to get to and from the shops. I assume there are buses.'

'There are buses but I could drive you. You'll probably have a lot of stuff to get and bringing it home in the car is easier than carting it home on a bus. After work tomorrow? We'd better check with Jean-Luc as he'll probably need to find a supermarket as well.'

Why was he doing this? Making arrangements that meant he would see more of her? Theo puzzled over this dilemma as they exited the park, a little part of him feeling regret that they'd not taken advantage of the night-time romantic ambience.

He must be crazy, although Jean-Luc would probably be with them the following day.

Jean-Luc? Grace was living in a flat above him. Surely he'd have been a better candidate for a sperm donation.

'Why not Jean-Luc?' Theo asked, as they waited for traffic to clear before crossing the road to the big old house that had been divided into flats and was kept by the hospital for visiting medical personnel. She turned to him, hesitated an instant, then offered him a smile that was only marginally better than a grimace. They crossed the road before she answered.

She turned to face him on the footpath outside the house. 'Believe it or not, I *did* consider it.' There was enough honesty in her voice for him to know it was the truth. 'But how embarrassing for both of us if he felt he didn't want to do it,' she continued, 'and probably worse if he did agree. No, it had to be someone a little more at arm's length, if you know what I mean. Anyway, thanks to your common sense I've realised I was being unduly optimistic and definitely irrational in thinking I could do it my way. I'll get in touch with an IVF clinic here and find out what's involved in getting on a programme.'

Clinics, hospitals, how impersonal a way to conceive a child. In his mind he pictured this beautiful but basically, he suspected, shy woman, sitting in a waiting room with other anxious women, talking to the professionals, trying to act nonchalant while burning up with embarrassment.

'Look,' he said, aware he should be running a mile yet caught up in her situation against his better judgement. 'Don't do anything just yet. Your father's birthday's not until the end of the year, you said. There's time. Let me think.'

She turned towards him, frowning now.

'I don't want you doing anything for me out of pity,' she snapped. 'I know I've made a fool of myself this evening but that doesn't mean I can't organise my own life. *And* the conception of my own child, should I decide to go ahead.'

He had to smile and without thinking he reached up and brushed the last of the flowers out of her short, fair hair.

'I thought that was just what you couldn't do,' he teased, but so gently he was sure she wouldn't take offence.

Which she didn't—just standing there, staring at him, the blue eyes brighter than ever.

With unshed tears?

He couldn't tell and he certainly wasn't going to ask.

But neither did he want her going into her empty flat so obviously upset. For some obscure reason this practical, efficient, usually composed woman brought out all his protective instincts.

'I'll see you tomorrow. We'll shop. You organise it with Jean-Luc—ask if he wants to join us.' He hoped talking practicalities would help and, indeed, she did seem better, for she straightened up and nodded, then agreed she'd speak to Jean-Luc.

As he strode away up the road, Grace leant on the rickety wooden gate, watching him go, waiting for the stupid tears that had gathered in her eyes to go away before she went inside.

She hadn't taped him as a kind man, but that's what he'd turned out to be. Unfortunately, kindness was something she couldn't handle very well. She was OK when *she* was being kind. In fact, she liked helping people—even people who didn't realise they needed help, her father said—but being on the receiving end, that unnerved her, made her suspicious, wondering what the person being kind might want of her.

Not that Theo would want anything. From the little she knew of him, she sensed he was one of those people who were sufficient unto themselves, not needing outside entertainment, or company, or even a close companion.

She pushed open the gate, aware she was making assumptions that had absolutely no basis in fact. How could she be making such a judgement on a man she barely knew?

But he *had* been kind…

# CHAPTER THREE

THEO sat by Scarlett Robinson's crib, watching her chest rise and fall, trying to work out how much of the work her lungs were doing and how much the machine. She'd seemed stronger earlier today and he'd adjusted the flow through the ECMO machine, knowing her heart and lungs would grow stronger if they had to do the work themselves.

But had he made too big an adjustment?

Were the drugs she needed already affecting other organs?

Was fluid collecting in her abdomen?

It didn't seem so. According to the monitors she was doing well, but for how long?

'It always seems terrible to me that we have to wait for another child to die so we can save one.'

He turned, startled by the voice in the night-quiet of the PICU, and even more startled by whose voice it was.

'What *are* you doing here?' he demanded, as Grace pulled a chair close so she, too, could sit and look at Scarlett.

'Can you ask that question when you told me you were coming back up to the hospital to get your car?'

She didn't look at him, her gaze focussed on the baby, not hungrily but with so much longing Theo had to wonder again if she was being totally honest with herself, or with him, talking of the baby she wanted as a gift for her father.

He turned so he could see her face and she lifted one shoulder in a shrug.

'It's a habit of mine. Early on, when I first worked paeds, my supervisor told me in no uncertain terms that to get too attached to the babies and children was a sure way to lose focus on the work.'

She sighed, then continued, 'And I think he was right to a certain extent, but I found I needed to know them better—to know them as people rather than bed numbers or HLHSs or whatever—so I got into the habit of coming in at night to check on them, sometimes sit with them for a while.'

'Coming in at night so you didn't spoil your emotionally detached image?' Theo queried, and she straightened up and shot him a glacial look.

'I can take an interest without becoming emotionally attached to a patient. It's just that someone, seeing me here, might think the way you obviously do and I don't want people getting the wrong impression. It's so hard to get into paeds cardiac surgery, especially as a woman, that I can't afford to put a foot wrong.'

'And being an unmarried mother wouldn't be putting a foot wrong?'

'These days?' she scoffed. 'I think intelligent people have moved beyond such prejudice. But that's what's so good about getting pregnant while I'm in Australia. Here I'm a stranger so no one knows my personal background and even if they do find out about the pregnancy they will assume it's something to do with an ongoing relationship back home. And going home pregnant, well, that's the easy part. People will assume I had a love affair in Australia and while they may be surprised that such a thing happened to a person like me, it will be a nine-day wonder then another bit of gossip will take its place and life will go on.'

Theo stared at her.

'Are you really so detached? Do you believe the things you say? Believe you won't be hurt by gossip and innuendo?'

She turned to face him, her defiance easy to read, but he suspected that behind it lay pain—pain that she'd learned to hide.

'I won't be hurt,' came the fierce reply. 'Neither will my child.'

He believed her about the child—she'd be like a lioness in protecting her offspring, but it was almost as if she accepted the hurt she might suffer herself.

Because she'd suffered hurt before?

That was the likely answer, but would he ever know? She was a strange woman.

'She needs a heart soon, doesn't she?'

The remark signalled the end of the conversation, but although he was willing to admit that this was hardly the place to be discussing personal matters, he wasn't finished with this conversation. Sitting with this woman, watching her with the very sick child, he could almost feel her longing for a child of her own.

'It's not just for your father, this baby, is it?' he asked, and she looked at him again.

'I don't want to talk about it,' she said. 'Don't you realise I feel a hundred kinds of fool already, just asking you? If you don't want to do it, that's fine, and I hope you find it in you to keep it to yourself that I did ask, but if you want to spread it around the hospital, well, I'll live with that.'

She stood up, and began to move away, but he caught her hand then dropped it as a nurse came in to do Scarlett's obs.

He followed Grace out to the lift foyer, standing beside her, trying to work out what must have happened to this woman to make her so defensive, yet so expectant of hurt. Except she'd deny that gossip about her would hurt—she already had, telling him she could live with it.

Which meant she'd had practice—but why? She was beautiful and intelligent—a little abrasive maybe, but many doctors and even more specialists had abrasive tendencies.

'I haven't said I won't do it,' he told her, as they entered a—thankfully empty—lift.

'What do you mean by that?'

'I mean I want to get to know you better. You may be thinking of me as an anonymous donor, but I don't want to father a child who might be neglected, or ill treated, not that I think you'd do that, but you must admit, your reason for wanting a child—as a present for your father—is a bit suspect.'

She stared at him, opened her mouth, no doubt to protest, then shut it again and shook her head, frowning so fiercely he wondered if he'd completely squashed the idea. But again that valiant side of her he thought he'd seen before rallied.

'Of course,' she said. 'You're right. It would be irresponsible of you not to check, although I imagine if you donated sperm at a sperm bank you'd only have their word that the child would be going to a good home.'

His turn to frown.

'I have no intention of donating sperm to a sperm bank,' he growled, wondering how this woman could tie him into knots so easily.

'Of course not,' she said, exiting the lift on the ground floor, 'but the analogy is there surely. You'd have to trust that the people at the sperm bank would do their homework and act responsibly. So what do you want? I've references with me, both personal and professional, and I've a plan for child care. Margie, the woman who helped my father care for me, still lives in my home and although she's now too old to care for an infant full time, she'll be an ideal granny and she has a niece who trained in child care and has nannied all around the world. I know she'd like to come home so I thought I'd use her, but I want to be a hands-on mother as well, so as far as possible I'll work around the baby and later the child.'

Grace stopped and looked at Theo, wondering if this was what he wanted, feeling acutely uncomfortable— well, that was natural considering the conversations they kept having—but a little bit hopeful as well.

'Is that the kind of thing you want to know? Or financial things? I could get my bank to contact you. I have my own home, no mortgage.'

He made an exasperated noise, grabbed her by the elbow and all but dragged her outside, guiding her through the car park and finally stopping by a silver four-wheel drive.

'No, that's not the kind of thing I want to know,' he muttered. 'Didn't you hear yourself, rattling off the perfect upbringing for a child, totally devoid of any emotional input at all? That's what bothers me—the idea of a child conceived for the sole purpose of being a gift, brought up according to rules and books. Oh, I don't doubt he or she will have a perfect life, but where does love come in?'

'Love?'

The word faltered from her lips, his question so bizarre she could only stare at him.

'Have you never felt love? Or if not love, at least lust?' he grumbled. 'Never felt *some* kind of emotion?'

And with that he drew her closer, put his hand to the back of her head and bent to kiss her. Or was it a kiss? Their lips certainly met, but his were hard and angry, hot and demanding, dragging a response from her so her mouth opened and his tongue invaded it, as bold as a conqueror taking a foreign land.

Was she really thinking such weird thoughts?

And why *was* she responding?

Because her body wasn't answering her brain's commands. Her brain was certainly telling her to push him away, to move, to run if necessary, but her body seemed to be enjoying the assault.

Eventually it was he who moved, lifting his head and breathing deeply, looking up at the night sky, not at her, the only sound from him a contemplative 'Hmm'.

After which he unlocked his car, opened the passenger side door, said, 'I'll drive you home,' and waited for her to climb in. She was no sooner seated than he reached across her with the seat belt, snapping it home, and although she protested that she was perfectly capable of doing up her own seat belt, he ignored the feeble words, striding around the hood and climbing into the vehicle beside her.

They were sitting at the hospital gates, waiting for the lights to change, when Theo spoke. 'We're shopping tomorrow, I know, but after that, the next evening, if you're not on duty, I'll cook dinner for us at my place. I am not yet committing myself to your audacious plan, but if you want me to think about it, you must grant me the pleasure—is pleasure the word I need?—of getting to know you better.'

'Well, of all the—'

Grace bit off the protest she was about to make. The man was Greek—it was in his blood to want to be the boss—and it certainly sounded as if he might be considering agreeing to her proposition, although she didn't think the kissing part was necessary. That was something she'd have to think about later when she was away from the distraction his body—and the memory of the kiss—was causing her.

No, what she had to do now was remain detached—not get too hopeful.

Theo eyed her suspiciously. He'd expected her to rebel against such high-handed treatment, and she'd begun to protest, but the words had died on her lips.

Keeping on side with him—he could practically hear her reasoning. But that was OK. What really bothered him was his own behaviour. First kissing the woman, and now making arrangements to see more of her. Surely he wasn't really thinking of helping her out?

And that's all it would be! The pain of losing little Elena had been so great he knew he could never live through it again—and the only way to ensure that was to not have another child.

Although a child that was yet wasn't his? It could work! He could watch from afar—be involved in that he was kept informed of the child's progress, and make joint decisions about important things like education. He'd certainly want that much. Just no emotional attachment! And that's what Grace would not only understand but was insisting on.

In fact, a child like this could be the perfect solution to the inheritance problem he had, although if the child became his heir, he or she would eventually become a very wealthy person, so it would be his responsibility to make sure the child could handle such a situation.

Which meant he would have more responsibility towards the child than he would really want...

But couldn't he handle that without emotional attachment?

Surely it would be possible, especially if the child grew up on another continent! It was just a matter of putting some safeguards in place and overseeing things like the child's upbringing and education. From a distance, of course.

He ignored a queasy feeling in his stomach, putting it down to remembered pain from Elena's death. He was being practical here—practical, detached and unemotional, like a scientist in search of a solution to a particular problem.

Suddenly the idea had possibilities, although, as often with the very best of ideas, there were issues that couldn't be ignored.

'Is it fair on the child?'

He'd pulled up outside her flat and hadn't really intended to ask the question, but the thought kept sneaking into his head and had escaped without him being fully aware of it.

'Is what fair on the child?' she asked, turning towards him so in the light from a streetlamp he could see the lower part of her face quite clearly—see the slightly fuller lips he'd kissed only minutes earlier...

Tasted...

He dragged his mind back to the conversation.

'To grow up without a father?'

She scowled at him.

'Give me a break! Take a look at statistics. Nearly half the children growing up in so-called civilised countries are growing up in single-parent households, having perhaps occasional contact with the non-custodial parent. Those kids don't all turn into axe murderers, you know. Most of them are fine. I grew up without a mother and I managed.'

Did you? Theo wanted to say, but he didn't, afraid it might hurt her, but he couldn't help but wonder if it was growing up without a mother's love that made her so detached—so defensive.

So desperate to mother a child of her own?

And once again, thinking of the little motherless girl-child Grace would have been, she sneaked beneath his defences, so when he touched her on the shoulder his hand was gentle, and when he said, 'Let's take it one day at a time, for the moment,' he hoped she'd understand that he was seriously considering helping her out, although he had grave doubts about purely clinical sperm donation. Given the attraction he felt towards her, there was, and always had been, a better way…

Was he weakening? Grace wondered as she stood in the shadowed porch outside the front door and watched his taillights disappear up the road. And if he was, how did she feel about it?

'Far from happy about the getting-to-know-you-better part,' she muttered to herself, lifting her fingers to her lips and feeling where he'd kissed.

But he'd kissed her to prove a point—quite what point she wasn't sure. But it had certainly been a proving-a-point kiss, not a getting-to-know-you kiss.

She laughed at herself as she unlocked the front door—who was she to be even attempting to classify kisses? It had been so long since she'd experienced a kiss she'd forgotten what one felt like.

Certainly not hard and hot and demanding, she was sure.

Scarlett's condition was deteriorating. Theo didn't need Alex's words to tell him, although Alex was explaining to all the team at the morning ward round how fluid was accumulating in her belly.

'Will you draw some off?' Grace asked, giving Theo the opportunity to look openly at her, not stealthily sideways as he had been doing throughout the round.

Why the idea of an heir hadn't occurred to him when

Grace had first mooted her sperm-donation idea he couldn't say, but since it had struck him as a possibility last night he'd thought of little else, conveniently ignoring a hidden uneasiness that questioned the emotional detachment rationale. Suddenly he had a way out of a dilemma that had become so great he'd forced himself to stop thinking about it. His father's will stipulated that only a child of his bloodline could inherit so although Theo himself would have been more than happy to give away the money—to hospitals and congenital heart disease research institutions—he was tied.

In fact, he'd resigned himself to the money going to his father's younger brother's family, a mob of wastrels if ever there was one. They'd already run through the money *their* father had bequeathed to them and were forever applying to Theo for what they euphemistically termed 'loans'.

Alex was explaining to Grace that they'd drawn off however many cc's of fluid the previous day, but more and more had built up.

'Less perfusion?' Grace suggested, and Alex turned to Theo, who put aside all private thoughts and concentrated on work.

'I'm concerned if we reduce the flow, which is already minimal—it could cause kidney damage. I've gone over all the material I can find on fluid build-up and believe it's leaking from her tissues rather than blood related, but we could try reducing the blood flow and increasing the oxygenation, which might protect the organs.'

'Or might not,' Phil said. 'What worries me is that she's on the transplant list but if a heart became available right now, here in this hospital, would we operate on her? Is she well enough? Could she take it?'

Theo looked at the pretty little baby girl lying in the crib, unaware of the life-or-death discussion going on around her. He prided himself on not getting emotionally involved with patients, but there was something special about this baby—this little girl.

And he knew the answer to Phil's questions—no, as Scarlett was today, they couldn't operate.

'Let's draw off more fluid, reduce the perfusion, do as you say, Theo, and add extra oxygen, and see what happens,' Alex decided, but Phil again halted the group before they moved on.

'Do we take her off the list?'

They all knew what list he was talking about. Children and adults needing donor hearts were listed on a central Australia-wide register and when a heart became available, it went to the next person on the list, according to its size and compatibility.

'And possibly let a heart that would suit her go to someone else?' Grace demanded.

'Better than waste it giving it to Scarlett then losing her and a viable heart that might have saved another child.'

Alex's registrar, Aldo Stephens, voiced the thought in everyone's mind, but Grace apparently didn't give in too easily—not that Theo should be surprised!

'We don't *know* she couldn't handle it,' she said. 'I've operated on very sick babies who have come through like little champions, and on top of that, who's to say a healthier baby will definitely survive a transplant op? I hate the idea of delisting Scarlett. She might be better tomorrow but would have to be relisted lower down. Surely we can wait until we're offered a heart and then make the decision about whether she's well enough or not. If we decide not, then the heart goes to the next on the list anyway and there's nothing but a really small period of time lost, but at least she can keep her place until then.'

Theo felt like giving a cheer, but Grace was looking embarrassed enough, perhaps thinking, as a newcomer to the team, she shouldn't have spoken so forcefully. Phil and Maggie both now backed her up and Alex nodded at least partial agreement.

'We'll keep her on another day and see how she responds to the changes in the ECMO. What's the level of the diuretics we're giving her, Aldo? Can we increase them without jeopardising anything else?'

The discussion turned to drugs, and although Grace was no doubt interested and taking it all in, her eyes were on Scarlett and Theo knew, for all she might deny it, she *did* get emotionally involved with her patients.

Which must augur well for her as a mother, surely, he decided.

But wasn't his thinking becoming clouded by the fact he found her attractive—as in he was undeniably attracted to her?

Which should have been reason enough to avoid her, but he could hardly call off the shopping trip as these people were colleagues—it was only polite to show them where they could shop.

Having Jean-Luc there made things easy. All Theo had to do was show them where the shopping trolleys were then guide them around the store. Although he did hear himself offering to push Grace's trolley.

'Push Jean-Luc's if you want to push a trolley,' she told him, marching down the refrigerator aisle at a mile a minute, lifting items off shelves, checking the labels and either rejecting or selecting them.

'A formidable woman,' Jean-Luc remarked as he stacked yoghurt into his trolley. 'Not many get into our specialty—I imagine it cost her a lot.'

And not for the first time Theo wondered just why such a beautiful woman was still unmarried at thirty-five. By choice, he was sure, but if she wanted a child surely a conventional marriage would have been the best way to produce one.

'Can you believe that man?' Grace said to Theo as they waited on the far side of the checkouts for the other doctor to finish. 'It took him five minutes to choose which coffee beans to buy, then he had to put the beans through the grinder, then get a coffee-pot.'

Theo said nothing but he understood why Grace had felt she couldn't ask Jean-Luc—the two of them were polar opposites. But the Frenchman did eventually finish his shopping, politely thanking them for waiting and inviting both of them to have coffee with him when they returned to his flat.

Interested in seeing Grace in a social environment, Theo agreed, although he would have preferred having coffee with Grace on her own, the attraction he was feeling towards her suggesting that making a baby with her might be a lot of fun.

Which was a very irresponsible thought!

But since the notion of the baby being a suitable heir

had occurred to him, he was interested in Grace's proposal on more than the attraction level, although he wasn't getting caught up in the idea until he knew a whole lot more about the woman who would be the baby's mother.

*And* until he'd thought through all the implications for the baby…

*His* baby!

The inner queasiness returned.

They were unloading groceries from the car when Lauren Henderson, a nurse in the PICU, arrived at the flats where the two surgeons were living. Theo knew her well, or as well as any fellow worker could know a very reserved woman. That she was there to see Jean-Luc was obvious, and that she was nervous, to the point almost of panic, was also evident to Theo.

But whatever was bothering her had to remain a mystery, for she left within minutes of arriving, an anxious-looking Jean-Luc going after her.

'It doesn't look as if we're going to get coffee here,' Grace said, turning off the hot plate under the coffee-pot. 'Shall we walk across the park and get some?'

Theo hesitated, and she smiled.

'I have no ulterior motive,' she said. 'I don't want romance in the shadows or further discussion on me wanting a child. I simply want a decent cup of coffee.'

He agreed and they crossed the road and entered the night-lit park, and though he'd walked through it in the evening many times, tonight it struck Theo that there was a romantic air about the place. Perhaps it was the thick shadows of the Moreton Bay fig trees, or the sound of the fountain splashing in the pond, or even the way you could see the stars in spite of the city lights…

'Why no romance, Grace?' he asked, an earlier thought recurring. 'I don't mean right here and now in the park, but in your life. You're a beautiful woman, there must have been men interested in you. Was there no one you wanted to settle down with and raise a family in what most would consider a normal way?'

She glanced his way but didn't answer, simply lengthening her stride as if she needed to get away, not only from him but from the question.

'You did ask *me* some very personal questions,' he reminded her, keeping up with her pace easily but finding it harder to guess at her mood.

'I was left at the altar,' she said, after several minutes of very tight silence. 'Literally! And if you've ever suffered any kind of humiliation—something I can't imagine you have—then arriving at a church where all your friends and colleagues are gathered, in full bridal regalia, to find that the groom has changed his mind would be, oh, I'd say a thousand times worse. Maybe a million. Or a trillion!'

She stopped walking and turned to face him.

'Of course, turning up at work a couple of weeks later—I'd taken time off for my honeymoon, would you believe—was easy after that.'

'*Sto diablo*! That happened to you? A man did that to you? And you don't want to—what? Castrate the lot of us? *Dio*, Grace, you must have the courage of a lion to have gone back to work and faced your friends and colleagues.'

She turned away as if embarrassed by his words,

then swung back to face him, and he read the pain in her face, but beyond the pain a strength of character that filled him with admiration.

'That man had devastated my personal life,' she said, her face pale and set in the moonlight that filtered through the leaves of the tree beneath which they stood. 'He'd killed my dreams of a perfect life with a husband and a family, but there was no way on earth I'd let him harm my professional one. So, of course, I had to go back, pretending to not hear the whispers, ignoring the snickers and the jibes.'

She gave a shrug and offered Theo the saddest smile he'd ever seen.

'It was a long time ago—I'm over it now,' she said, but he knew she wasn't—knew she'd never trust another man again. Knew, also, why she'd shut herself off from what was considered normal small talk and gossip—things at which all hospitals excelled. The story would have circulated for months and she'd had to work in an atmosphere of snide remarks and hidden sniggers.

He put his hands on her shoulders and drew her close, wrapping her in a gentle hug.

'It explains why you want a stranger's baby,' he said gently, his cheek resting against her soft hair, the delicate perfume—was it really something as simple as orange blossom?—of her shampoo tickling his nose.

She rested her body against his for a moment, sighing with the night breeze, then she eased away.

'Coffee,' she said, as calmly as if she hadn't just ripped out her heart and offered it to him for his inspection.

What could he say? He turned to walk beside her, and when he put his arm around her waist she didn't shrug it away, suggesting she needed comfort after her confession, although he knew she'd never have asked for it. Not from him or any man—except perhaps her father…

Was it he who'd helped her through that time?

Of course it would have been—he would have been with her, leading her to the altar!

In that case she had extra reason to want to please him with a grandchild…

'Tell me about your home,' he suggested, when they were seated in the courtyard of the brasserie again, cups of coffee in front of them.

'My home?' she repeated, as if the words were hard to understand.

'Where you live,' Theo prompted, and finally saw her smile, a genuine smile, warmed by happier memories.

'It's on the edge of the city, near vineyards. I have an acre of land that Margie's husband kind of looks after. In actual fact, he hires gardeners to come in to cut the grass and trim the hedges but he still grows the most wonderful vegetables, and I have fruit trees, peaches and apples and a cherry tree that never fruits but is so pretty I haven't the heart to cut it down. Margie and her husband live in the house with me and my father lives up the road, not far away.'

She paused and he knew from the peaceful look on her face and the slight smile on her lips that she was picturing her home.

'We look out to the mountains. They're quite close,

and beautiful. There are riding trails so if the child wants a pony, that would be fine.'

'You rode there with your father?' Theo guessed, and Grace nodded, the smile gathering strength as better memories surfaced.

'Still do when we both have time, although it's rare these days. But he keeps our horses at his place and has them cared for and exercised regularly.'

She paused and looked at him, the blue eyes watching him as if to gauge his reaction to something she was unsure about saying.

'I told you I wanted a grandchild for my father, but that's mostly because I didn't want you to think I wanted to get pregnant for silly or sentimental reasons, but I know I have so much to offer a child, Theo. I've got a lot of unused love for a start, and a wonderful place to live where a child can be a child, running in the garden, riding, climbing the hills, learning how things work and grow...'

How could someone have jilted her like that? Theo wondered, seeing the blue eyes shining with memories and ideas—with the love she'd lavish on a child! She might be a bit abrupt, but she was beautiful.

And sexy.

Should he put *his* proposition to her?

Suggest now that maybe the regular, proven and enjoyable way of making babies would be—what? More fun?

He doubted she'd go for that. She was a woman who had relegated fun to a very low priority in her life.

Although if he convinced her that the regular way had more chance of being successful?

That might work, but was he being fair? He didn't want her accepting his advances purely for the sake of a baby. Well, he did, but surely it wouldn't hurt to make the most of the attraction he felt, and which he was sure was reciprocated, at the same time.

'You've stopped listening,' she said, and he had to admit she was right.

'It wasn't that interesting anyway,' she continued, 'although having asked me about my home, you could at least have pretended to listen.'

'What a contrary woman you are! You put yourself down and at the same time tear a strip off me. I *was* listening—riding trails and mountains and your father keeps the horses. But I was thinking at the same time.'

'About my suggestion? Would you be willing?'

She was so obviously excited he hated to squelch it, so he said, 'With some reservations—or perhaps revisions would be a better word—yes.'

'Revisions?'

She wasn't stupid—she'd picked up on the crux of the matter right away.

'We'll talk about them on the way home,' he said, standing up, then holding her chair for her as she stood.

How long since a man who wasn't my father did that for me? Grace wondered, pleased by the gesture but worried about these so-called 'revisions' Theo had mentioned. How on earth could you revise a sperm donation?

But as they strolled through the park, she began to suspect, for Theo's arm, slung so casually around her shoulders as they'd crossed the road, was now drawing her closer to his body, his hand trailing lightly up and down her arm, making her nerves tingle with awareness.

'In France,' he murmured, drawing her into the deeper shadows of a huge tree, 'they have a saying for when two people meet and are attracted to each other. They say their atoms hooked.'

He turned her so he was looking down into her face, and she was thankful for the shadows so he wouldn't see the colour in her cheeks—brought on by uncertainty, not prudishness. And now he brushed his lips across her mouth in a questioning kiss.

'Am I wrong in thinking ours have hooked?' he murmured.

She didn't pull away, but neither did she agree, aware he was correct in his assumption, yet very, very wary.

This wasn't what she'd wanted.

In fact, it was the last thing she wanted, although she understood now Theo's talk of revisions.

And the problem was they made sense. Wouldn't having sex with Theo give her a better chance of conceiving than messing around with some kind of artificial insemination—the logistics of which she hadn't fully worked out?

The kiss deepened—well, she hadn't indicated that he *couldn't* kiss her, had she?—and she found herself responding. Very tentatively moving her lips, even more cautiously touching her tongue to his. Memories of Paul's derision were hammering in her head, hateful, hurtful taunts coming back to haunt her.

'I'm not very good at this,' she muttered against Theo's lips, so softly she rather hoped he wouldn't hear.

But hear he must have, for he set her roughly aside and stared down into her face, a stream of what she could only imagine were Greek profanities issued from his mouth.

# CHAPTER FOUR

THEO drove slowly up the road towards the hospital, clenching his hands on the steering-wheel so he'd feel the tightness in the skin and tendons burned in the accident, needing the reminder of why he didn't want to get emotionally involved again.

Not ever!

And not getting emotionally involved meant not feeling sorry for Grace Sutherland when she came out with things that made him realise how badly the rat who'd left her at the altar had hurt her. Only with Grace the scars were too deep to see. Deeply hidden behind her cool composure and her slightly acid tongue. Yes, her remote manner was definitely a defence, like a suit of armour she wore to protect her from further injury.

That he had his own protective armour didn't bother him in the least—that was different. He was a man but, understanding, he could respect her defences.

He parked his car in a short-term doctors' space, wanting only to see how Scarlett was coping on the reduced flow rate. He'd have been paged if there were any problems, but nothing, in his experience, beat seeing for himself.

He was surprised to see the woman sitting by the crib, then pleased that Scarlett's mother had managed to get down to Sydney once again. She stood up as he arrived, explaining that she'd been beside the baby all afternoon and was going to get some sleep now but her husband would be in to sit with Scarlett shortly.

'You've managed to both get down, then?' Theo said, delighted for them and for the baby.

Mrs Robinson smiled.

'Some wonderful person donated money through the hospital social work department to pay a couple who do relief work for farmers to stay on the farm. The wife— we know her because she worked on the farm next door—will look after the kids and her husband will keep an eye on the stock. My mum's there as well so she's overseeing things. As soon as we knew the couple were coming we flew straight down—there was money for our air fares and expenses as well. Wasn't it fantastic?'

Theo agreed that it was indeed fantastic, but his attention was focussed on the little baby who lay so still, only partially conscious as she was sedated to prevent movement so her little body wasn't using any excess energy. But when Theo bent over her crib, her eyes were open, the dark opaque blue of newborns, and they moved, seeming to focus on his face. He smiled at her and said her name, quietly, aware she was too young to recognise it, or faces, but needing the contact.

Her notes showed her oxygen values were good in spite of the decreased flow, and, looking at her little belly, it seemed less bloated.

'Good girl,' he told her. 'You just hang in there and we'll get you a heart. Tomorrow you'll have scans and an ultrasound to make sure everything's OK, but you're still on the list, poppet, thanks to Dr Sutherland.'

He sat down, thinking of Grace. Not about her request that he father her child—he'd already decided to do that and, having decided, would go ahead in his own way, certain to be pleasurable. But what he had to think about was how Grace might react to his decision to take an interest in the child.

From afar, of course…

Unemotionally…

Grace lay in bed, thinking of Theo Corones. More accurately, thinking of Theo Corones's kiss.

*And* the effect it had had on her body!

That his revisions meant he wanted her to conceive her child the normal way she had no doubt, but although he, being a man, could have sex with any woman to whom he was attracted without becoming emotionally involved, could she?

Could any woman?

She realised she couldn't speak for other women, although in this day and age she knew some women had sex in the same way men did—for fun and pleasure and with no emotional entanglements at all. So that wasn't the question. *Her* question was, could she? Not for fun and pleasure, but for a baby.

Of course she could!

She *had* to!

And she turned her pillow over, seeking a cool spot

on the pillow slip, and found herself thinking once again of Theo's kiss. And of how it had made her feel…

Up early the next day, she showered and prepared to dress for work. Which was where her upbeat mood faltered. For years she'd dressed in sensible shirts and skirts or tailored trousers, promoting an image of classic efficiency, but today her shirt seemed drab, while her skirt made her look like an old maid.

'You are an old maid!' she reminded herself, frowning at her image in the mirror.

'But you needn't look like a staid old maid,' she muttered, going back to her cupboard and looking through the very sensible clothes she'd brought with her to Australia. Practical clothes, work clothes—sensible…

'What the hell is wrong with me? One kiss—well, maybe more than one—a sensible discussion on procreation, and I'm getting all het up over my wardrobe.'

But she pulled off the skirt and pulled on a pair of black trousers, frowned at herself as they were evening trousers. The white linen? Better than the black but hardly practical for work. She sighed, returning to the skirt—navy denim, eminently sensible, but perhaps if she left open the top button of her white shirt she'd look less…

Strait-laced?

Uptight?

She sighed again and pressed her fingers to her lips, thinking again of Theo's kisses and knowing they were the last thing she should have been thinking about.

Downstairs she tapped on Jean-Luc's door but he

must have departed while she had been struggling with her clothing choices, so she walked up the road to the hospital on her own, wondering if the queasy feeling in her stomach when she thought about Theo was to do with the practical issues of procreation or the way his kisses made her feel.

He wasn't with the group gathered for the ward round—was she relieved or was the twinge she felt regret?—but as today was an operating day she imagined he'd be in Theatre, preparing his machine.

'Right,' Phil said cheerfully when the ward round was finished. 'My lot are starting in the cath lab, where we're going to do a balloon valvuplasty to open up the pulmonic valve so young Brett Scott can get better blood flow to his lungs. Grace, as we discussed yesterday, you're the main man and I'll be explaining to the students as we all watch the monitor.'

Grace followed Phil towards the small room used for these procedures, wondering how the group of students accompanying them would all fit in.

'They don't,' Phil explained, when she voiced her doubts. 'They watch it on a second monitor in another room, but I'll be with you, explaining the procedure as you go. We used to do the cath and explain at the same time, but Alex decided that wasn't fair on the patient to have even a small portion of the operator's attention not on the actual job.'

'Suits me,' Grace told him, checking the equipment already laid out for her, measuring the flexible steel tubes that she'd ease into the blood vessel and steer up to the heart, checking the monitors, second catheter they'd use to place a guide wire, the balloons of different sizes which they would inflate to open up the valves.

All was ready. Brett was brought in, and the operation began, Phil talking from the end of the table, explaining that quite often the operation was performed by paediatric cardiologists rather than surgeons, the work carried out in cath labs in their surgeries, but that Brett was here because his cardiologist believed the valve might be particularly tough and would need expert help.

As he talked, Grace was threading the first wire in, a fluoroscope showing her on a monitor where the wire was at all times. Once into the heart, she had to measure the blood pressure in the right ventricle, beneath the valve, then in the pulmonary artery, above the valve. A tiny transducer on the catheter tip did this for her, displaying the pressures on a second monitor, giving her a valve gradient against which she could check the success of the operation later on.

'Now Grace will measure the size of the ring of tissue that holds the valve,' Phil explained to the students in the other room, while Grace asked for an injection of contrast—thick clear fluid that showed up dark on the fluoroscope—into the right ventricle. Filmed with a high speed camera as it passed through the heart, the contrast enabled her to work out the size of the ring she had to stretch, and then choose the correct balloon size.

Satisfied she had all the information she needed, she carefully withdrew the first catheter and began the second part of the operation, to place a guide wire into the pulmonary artery to steady the final catheter while she inflated the balloon.

Forty minutes later she was done, three inflations of the balloon opening up the valve enough for a final check of pressures below and above the valve proving very satisfactory.

'Well done,' Phil said to her as she stood at one side of the room, stripping off her gloves then removing her goggles and mask. 'You work so calmly and efficiently—although I don't know why I should be surprised. Everything about you suggests calm efficiency.'

Including my clothes, Grace thought to herself, not at all happy with the compliment Phil had given her, although all her years in medicine this was exactly the image she had tried to project.

It was Theo's fault, probing into her past, opening the door to the possibility of an affair, making her body feel things she didn't want to feel and her mind fear where such feelings might lead.

Panic overwhelmed her, to such an extent that when she ran into Theo in the tearoom a little later, she couldn't stop herself from speaking.

'I think I'd prefer a straight donation and maybe more than one if that doesn't do the trick, rather than revisions.' She blurted out the words then, belatedly, looked around, wondering just who else might have heard this weird declaration. Aldo was over by the window, working on his laptop, and from the look on his face nothing short of a bomb going off on the table next to him would disturb him.

He certainly hadn't looked up, neither did he move when Theo, one of his beautiful eyebrows raised, murmured, 'Is this really the right time and place?' at her.

She shrugged her shoulders, as awkward as a schoolgirl. 'It just came out,' she muttered at him, turning away to fill the kettle although she wanted neither tea nor coffee, just needing to hide her scarlet cheeks from him.

Although she *had* meant what she'd said.

Reluctantly she turned back to face him, hoping her blush had faded, but instead of assuring him she meant it, even if she hadn't chosen the best place to voice her thoughts, she realised he was smiling.

It wasn't the condescending kind of smile Paul had used when she'd done something to embarrass herself, but a real, friendly smile—one that crept under her skin and made her feel warm with pleasure.

A smile causing pleasure?

This had to stop right now!

'I meant it,' she said, but it came out far more lamely than she wanted, her determination undermined by his smile.

Not any smile, of course—it was a really lovely smile, possibly the first she'd seen from Theo. And if he was handsome when he was being Greek and fairly grim, Theo smiling went far beyond handsome.

And she needed her head read!

'I realise that,' he said, not smiling now. 'But the regular way of conception is so much easier—for me certainly. In fact, I'm not at all sure I could manage any other way. And on top of that, given the attraction you must admit exists, isn't it a good way for us to get to know each other better?'

Having been distracted by the smile, it took a moment for Grace to realise what he was saying, and she looked with horror at where Aldo had been sitting.

'He left while you were pretending to fill the kettle,' Theo said, and although she felt hugely relieved she was also irritated that she was so transparent.

'He wouldn't have known what we were talking about anyway,' she said, trying desperately to shore up her defences—trying to ignore the hot, excited feeling Theo's words had caused deep within her body. She latched on to an earlier bit of his conversation. 'And I thought any man would know how to...'

She knew cool, detached women, especially doctors, should be able to say the word in a cool, detached manner, but when it came to the crunch she choked on it.

'Masturbate?' Theo finished for her—so cool and detached himself she could have hit him, especially as she could feel fire in her cheeks yet again.

'Yes!' she said, although it made her even more embarrassed that he'd read her with ease.

'I might not want to, and I do think we should get to know each other better. Wouldn't you think it irresponsible of me to father a child if I didn't know the mother?' he asked, subtly turning the onus back on her. Grace shook her head, wondering just how she, Super-Cool Sutherland, had got herself into such a ludicrous situation.

She was about to storm out of the tearoom when Theo's hand on her shoulder stopped her.

'We'll talk about it later,' he said.

'Later?' She knew she was frowning at him, and as Phil and Maggie had just walked through the door she shouldn't be.

'Dinner, my place, tonight. I'll call for you at seven, OK?'

'Oh, lucky you!' Maggie said. 'Theo's house is to die for and on top of that the man can cook.'

Grace opened her mouth then realised that anything she might say would sound pathetic and closed it again.

She nodded at Theo and escaped, but as she scurried along the corridor she bumped into Lauren Henderson, and all the contrary emotion she'd been feeling suddenly focussed on the dissatisfaction she'd felt as she'd dressed for work that morning—on her clothes.

'Lauren, you're a local. Where would I shop for clothes?'

Lauren seemed surprised then she smiled as she glanced down at her own faded jeans and T-shirt.

'As you can see, I'm not that into clothes shopping, but you know the shopping centre Theo took you to last night?'

Grace nodded.

'Well, there are two or three boutiques there. I know Maggie shops there and she always looks great.'

There was a slight hesitation then Lauren added, 'Not that you don't always look great.'

Grace had to smile because Lauren was looking as embarrassed as Grace normally felt.

'I look neat,' she said, to soothe Lauren's kind heart. 'There's a difference.'

Lauren smiled.

'Neat's not in my vocabulary—not with a nine-year-old boy in the house. But you look more than neat, you look classy.'

They parted and although Grace knew she should be grateful to Lauren for the 'classy' compliment, she knew it was just another word for the cool, sophisticated image she tried to project—dull and boring fitted just as well.

Neat!

She found a cab outside the hospital and told the driver where she wanted to go, trying hard not to analyse why she was doing this, assuring herself she could look at clothes without buying any.

Without buying any? Two hours later she was in another cab, half a dozen pristine white shopping bags on the seat beside her. Fortunately there was no sign of Jean-Luc in their common foyer and she was able to escape up to her flat without having to discuss her shopping expedition. And she hadn't been in Sydney long enough for anyone to know much about her wardrobe, apart from work-wear, so no one—read Theo—would know that her reckless purchase of not one but two pairs of designer jeans and four new shirts—satin is the new black, madam—had been made because she'd panicked about going to his house for dinner.

Fortunately for her sanity—she was really beginning to wonder just why she'd needed new clothes—she had no time to ponder. In fact, she had barely enough time to shower and change.

She changed into one of the new pairs of jeans, black and skinny legged, making her own legs seem endless, especially when she added a pair of high-heeled sandals she'd bought at the last minute.

A white shirt with thin black stripes—justified in the shop because it would go with both her black skirt and her white slacks—completed the new dramatic outfit. She brushed her hair, touched her face with make-up, glossed her lips, then, feeling half excited and half foolish, hurried downstairs so she would be waiting when Theo arrived. Heaven forbid he came in and saw all her not-yet-unwrapped parcels. He would get totally the wrong idea.

Wouldn't he?

Theo double-parked outside Grace's place, and leaned over to open the door.

'Thanks for being ready, and I'm sorry about not getting out to open the door. Getting a place to park around here is often impossible.'

He spoke the apology automatically, watching the traffic around him, the man in the car behind gesturing impatiently, so it wasn't until he reached the traffic lights that he had time to turn and actually look at his companion.

'You look stunning.'

The words were out before he had time to consider either their impact on Grace or on why he should be surprised.

'I mean, you're a beautiful woman, you always look classy, but tonight…'

He let the sentence hang, his mind already miles ahead, wondering if she'd dressed up—could you call jeans and a shirt dressing up?—because she was reconsidering his 'revisions'?

His body tensed with excitement…

She didn't reply, simply leaned back in the seat and crossed her legs—legs that went on for ever—encased in black jeans, a strappy black sandal dangling negligently from her foot.

Had he misjudged her completely?

Was this elegantly sexy creature the real Grace?

And, if so, how had he come to be feeling sorry for such a beautiful woman?

'Is it far away, your place?'

Her question made him realise he'd been lost in specu-lation, and he explained how, although he lived in a neighbouring suburb, one-way streets made it seem further.

'I've a terrace house. For someone with a house on an acre of land it will seem minute to you. It was in a sad way when I bought it but I like working with my hands and I've enjoyed doing it up.'

Such normal-sounding conversation, Grace thought, wanting to ask him if DIY activities were a substitute for operating, wondering what she would do if she couldn't use her skill on babies, but he was doing the polite thing so well that she had to respond in the same way, pretend-ing they were newly met acquaintances and colleagues, not people who'd already discussed something as ri-diculously personal as the possible transfer of sperm.

The house looked like something out of a picture book, a two-storied stone cottage squashed in the middle of a row of attached cottages, all in various states of disrepair. But Theo's house stood out, the stones newly sand- or water-blasted so they had turned a dusky pink in the light from the streetlamp on the footpath. The top storey boasted a tiny veranda with in-tricate wrought-iron lacework painted a pristine white.

'Did it look as bad as the others when you bought it?' she asked, as Theo gave her his hand to help her from the car.

'Worse,' he said. 'I decided to start with the worst.'

'But you've only been with the team eight months,' someone said. 'Have you done all the work in that time?'

He was leading her through a minuscule front yard, paved with old cobblestones and decorated with huge urns and pots containing ferns and flowering annuals, so bright petunias spilled down the sides of one and lacy leaves spread outward from another.

'I've lived in Sydney for a few years now, working at the Children's Hospital before coming across to Jimmie's.'

It wasn't the first time she'd heard St James's Hospital referred to as Jimmie's but, being new, she'd felt uncertain about using this nickname, as if it was too familiar a thing for a stranger to do.

Theo was unlocking his door, and as he pushed it open she forgot about hospital nicknames and looked around in wonder. Yes, the house was small, but Theo had opened up the downstairs so it was all one big room. The floor was polished wood, gleaming with golden life, and on it he'd set just one rug, an old rug—the jewel-rich colours suggesting Persian—to designate the sitting space. Comfortable leather armchairs were grouped around it, and further in a round table held an arrangement of leaves and flowers she knew had come from his pots out the front.

Had he brought them in and arranged them because she was coming, or was he a man who liked having their beauty in his house all the time?

Uncertainty crept over her—a new uncertainty. This one nothing to do with hooked atoms and everything to do with the fact that as she got to know this man, she might find herself liking him.

A lot.

'Bedroom and bathroom upstairs—it's a bachelor pad, no room for visitors—and if you come this way, you'll see my latest project.'

He led her past a streamlined kitchen tucked against the back wall and out into a courtyard, enclosed by high brick walls. Vines grew up the walls and on the southern side she saw an apple tree espaliered to precise perfection.

'The work of a surgeon undoubtedly,' she said, trying for a joke as being in Theo's house—Theo's delightful house—was making her more and more uncomfortable.

'I enjoy doing it,' he said, shrugging off her comment. 'Do sit.'

He indicated a padded bench, set under a pergola against the back wall of the house. Beside it was a table, a bottle of wine standing in an ice-bucket and, beneath a fine muslin cloth, obviously the makings of their dinner.

'Barbeque,' he explained. 'But not the traditional Aussie steak and sausages, unless, of course, you don't eat salmon. I do have steak.'

'Fresh salmon, I love it. Hate cooking it because it makes the kitchen smell.'

'Which is why I always barbeque it,' he said, his lips twitching so much she frowned at him.

'What?' she demanded, and he finally gave in and laughed.

'Oh, Grace,' he said, when his laughter stopped, but a smile remained in his voice. 'Do you hear us? Prattling on about cooking smells while in the back of both our minds are things of such magnitude salmon smells are the least of our worries.'

He paused, then added, still smiling at her, 'It's how we're brought up, isn't it? Politeness at all costs! Don't talk about anything that's inappropriate—and sex definitely comes into the "don't talk about it" category. So we go through life talking about nothing in particular, while in our heads totally different conversations are going on.'

The smile made her uncomfortable—kind of squirmy inside—but not as uncomfortable as the things he'd said.

'I thought I was the only person in the world who had head conversations so totally different from my audible conversations they might come from different people.'

'No way—why should you have all the fun?' he said, so lightly she knew he was teasing her. But instead of upsetting her, as teasing usually did, it made the squirmy feeling worse.

'Mine aren't fun most of the time,' she muttered, distracted by her insides, although now she thought about it, it had been a long time since lunch so maybe she was just hungry?

Which made her feel much better, although when Theo's fingers brushed hers as he passed her a glass of wine, and the feeling intensified yet again, she was hard put to convince herself it was hunger.

Was her insecurity solely the result of the rat who'd jilted her? Theo wondered as he took the salmon out of the marinade and set it on the hot grill plate.

Or had growing up without a mother contributed? Grace obviously adored her father so he must have done the right thing by her, but without a mother to tell her she was pretty, to build up her self-esteem—was that where things had gone wrong?

She was talking now about Scarlett and the improvement in her condition, so he could watch the fish cook, join in the conversation, and still ruminate on what had made Grace the way she was.

He lifted the cooked salmon pieces off the barbeque, set them on plates, then put them on the table, lifting the protective cloth to reveal a leafy salad and a special potato salad his mother swore had been handed down in the family since biblical times.

'Help yourself,' he said, pushing both bowls towards her.

She did, then ate with relish, and as he ate he realised that, when she wasn't asking very intrusive questions, she was very restful company.

Undemanding.

He liked that in a woman.

He didn't get involved with colleagues—too complicated.

This wasn't exactly getting involved…

'That was delicious.'

Her voice startled him out of his reverie, which was just as well, because he didn't like where his thoughts had been leading. Although the idea of a child was becoming more and more appealing, what he had to do was keep the conception purely clinical.

Enjoyable, his body was sure it would be that, but clinical…

'Is that the oven?'

Had she just noticed his work in progress or was the

silence stirring her senses as much as it was stirring his? Although he *had* offered to show it to her earlier.

'It is,' he said, and she stood up and walked across to where he'd built the basic structure of his beehive-shaped oven. 'I need to render it both outside and inside so the surfaces are all smooth, then try it out.'

'Lovely shape,' she said, running her hands down the fat-bellied curve, and seeing her, a faint smile of pleasure on her face, her hands touching the bricks he'd touched, he wanted her with such fierce hunger he had to turn away.

He took the plates and dishes inside, and was going back to get the glasses and half-empty wine bottle when he saw she'd moved, this time over to his apple tree, examining the diamond patterns into which he'd trained it.

'May I see your hands?' she asked, such a bizarre question he held them out, palms upward, so she could inspect them.

She ran her fingers over the barely discernible scars, her touch as light as spiders' feet against his skin.

'Did the car catch fire?'

He couldn't speak. He wanted to be angry, no, furious, with her—for her prurient curiosity, her intrusion—then he realised it wasn't curiosity or intrusion, it was empathy prompting her questions. His worst hurt had been emotional, and *that* she understood.

'It did,' he said, then he removed his hands from hers and put them on her shoulders, drawing her closer, sliding his hands to her waist so she was imprisoned, very lightly, in his arms.

'But that was then, and this is now, and in furtherance of your desire to have a child I am now going to kiss you because, as you well know, there is one almost sure-fire way for you to get pregnant, and that is by having sex. Not tonight, we need to know each other better, but soon, Grace Sutherland, if we find we click—our atoms hook—then that's the way it will be.'

# CHAPTER FIVE

WAS she really standing in this courtyard, letting this man kiss her?

The thought had barely floated through Grace's brain when she realised it wasn't all one-sided, the kissing thing. She'd joined in, and was kissing him back. She tried to analyse her feelings, but how to analyse warmth that spread from her lips, skimming her breasts, slithering down to heat her belly, then slinking lower to pool between her thighs, making her feel tight and excited.

And could you analyse nerve-endings that seemed to be alive, jangling in her body so every cell felt alert, her flesh eager for the flood of new sensations she was feeling?

His arms tightened against her spine so her body was now pressed against his, fitting easily in a way hers and Paul's had never seemed to fit. Height, it was probably height, she thought muzzily, then a deep-throated growl reminded her she was kissing, not thinking, and she concentrated again on the kiss.

Which was now making her knees feel decidedly

weak, or was that just an excuse to lean against him, to
check the fit again? A fit so good that she was only too
aware of his arousal, but far from being put off, as once
she might have been, she found that hard core pressed
against her belly exciting.

Theo was right—sex was a time-honoured way of
conception and as long as she wasn't foolish enough to
let emotion enter into the equation, perhaps she *could*
enjoy sex with Theo.

'I've lost you.'

He was growling again, but words this time, and
drawing away.

'Not really. I was thinking about sex, which wasn't
far removed from kissing.'

And even as the words came out she wondered why
it was so easy to talk to Theo—to say things she'd never
have dreamt of saying to anyone, male or female.

Because there was no emotional involvement?

It had to be that.

'Sex with me, I hope,' he said, pressing his lips
against her temple in such a pleasant way she wanted
to lean on him again.

'Of course with you,' she snapped, frustrated that she
couldn't lean—well aware the slightest lean would have
them both kissing again, and who knew where that
would lead?

Not yet, Theo had said, although the way she felt
right now she regretted not protesting the delay earlier.

'Then that is good,' he murmured, brushing his lips
against hers before straightening himself. 'Shall we
visit Scarlett on our way back to your place?'

Grace was nodding, but Theo had a feeling she was

still lost in the kiss and the nod was purely automatic. That other night at the hospital, he'd seen another side of Grace, the side who would be mother to the child they might or might not have, and seeing her with the very sick little girl was important to Theo.

He may not want emotional connections with the child, but he would do everything in his power to make sure it had all the love a mother could provide.

'What's wrong?'

Had he stiffened, thinking of Lena, who'd been more than happy to pass the care of their baby to the staff, who'd even refused to breast feed because it might destroy her figure? Oh, she'd insisted little Elena be named for her, but after that she'd wanted as little as possible to do with their child.

'Not a thing,' he said, but he'd turned away from Grace and was leading the way back through the house, trying to shove the past back where he usually kept it, in a deep, dark corner of his mind.

It wasn't far to the hospital, but far enough for the silence that now lay between them to grow heavier by the minute. And though he could think of no way to break it—Grace deserved better than some trite remark about work or weather—he knew her insecurity would be telling her it was somehow her fault that things had changed between them.

'I have dark memories,' he finally admitted, pulling up in a short-stay parking bay outside Jimmie's. 'They surface at unexpected and often inappropriate times.'

He turned and ran his hand down her soft, shiny hair, adding, 'It was unfair on you that one popped up back there.'

Then he leant towards her and kissed her on the lips, surprised to find just touching his mouth to hers provided balm for his troubled soul.

Or perhaps forgetfulness—wasn't that what he needed? Temporary amnesia—to lose himself with Grace.

In Grace?

The idea was appealing more and more but he had to be careful. Feeling empathy with her—understanding her insecurities—could be dangerous…

She returned his kiss, still tentative—just how badly had that man hurt her?—but with such sweetness and trust he again heard danger signals clanging in his head.

Scarlett lay quietly in her crib, sleeping it seemed, the weather-beaten man in the recliner beside her also sleeping. One glance was enough to show her condition was unchanged, although Grace worriedly touched the baby's belly, muttering about distension and fluid.

'If a heart comes up and she's not well enough to have it, I'll feel guilty for not taking her off the list,' she said, sinking into a chair on the other side of the baby's crib, her eyes feasting on the tiny girl.

'Don't get off on guilt,' Theo told her. 'You were only one of a team that made that decision, it wasn't yours alone. And by the time a heart comes up she might be over whatever's causing the fluid build-up.'

'I'm not getting off on guilt, as you put it,' Grace snapped, not insecure at all. 'But looking at her now I think Alex was probably right in suggesting we delist her.'

'He's the head of the team, he could have done it,'

Theo reminded her. 'The problem is that we all get not attached but definitely involved with the babies we have in the PICU. The fact that there's a baby in a similar situation in a PICU in Melbourne or Perth doesn't have the same impact on us as a baby we're seeing, and treating, and, I suppose, rooting for is the only way to put it. Scarlett is *our* baby while the others are more hypothetical babies.'

Grace smiled. 'I like the idea of hypothetical babies,' she said, then she stood up. 'I've an early start tomorrow. I'll walk home from here.'

'No way. I'll drive you.'

He stood up so they were close together at the end of Scarlett's crib, so close Theo could feel all his atoms hooking.

'No, Theo, I want to walk. I need the fresh air and some thinking time, but so I can think productively, are we past the hypothetical as far as my baby goes?'

The clear blue eyes looked into his, not anxious but wary, as if ready for a rebuff.

'Let us take this slowly, I certainly can't consider making a child on a whim, which is why I talked about revisions—physical revisions but ethical ones as well. Getting to know you. And on top of that we need to think about the child.'

Her smile stayed in place, but uncertainty replaced the wariness in her eyes.

'It's not a whim on my part, I've really thought it through. And although we've never really discussed the revisions, I do understand what you mean. Although I should warn you, Paul always said I was about as much fun to go to bed with as a dead whale.'

Theo's gut clenched. Did she not realise what these comments did to him?

Or how much he'd like to kill the rat called Paul?

But he had to play it cool, for her sake, so he smiled at her and raised an eyebrow.

'And did he go to bed with many dead whales?'

This time the smile was genuine.

'You know, I never asked him!' She shook her head. 'You must think I'm stupid, still worrying about things like that. Even *I* think I'm stupid. Surely an intelligent woman should have worked through it by now and moved on. In a way I have, but only by avoiding getting close to anyone—by avoiding relationships altogether. And, as you must know, that's not hard when you work the hours we do.'

'I still won't let you walk home alone. If you want the walk I'll walk with you, and if you want to think, I won't say a word.'

But you'll be there, Grace wanted to protest, but she could hardly say that it was him she wanted to think about—him and the way he made her feel, all alive and excited but at the same time fearful. Her body may be excited but trepidation at where her feelings might lead hung like dark, mysterious shadows in her head.

He walked her home, Grace's body so aware of his presence it grew more and more tense until an accidental brush of his hip against hers made her start.

'Twitchy!' he said, and she could hear the amusement in his voice.

'Is it always like this?' she found herself asking.

'What always like what?'

He was teasing her but she was getting used to it—

and sometimes she wondered if she might get to enjoy it—but now when she was so uptight she was worried the slightest touch might make her crack apart.

'You know what I mean,' she muttered. 'Atoms hooking, as you keep saying. Is it always so—so taut?'

'Taut is good,' he murmured, opening her front gate and taking her hand to lead her into the shade of a huge camellia bush by the front path. 'Taut means our bodies are communicating, taut means you'll need release and the best release of all is…'

Theo hesitated. He'd been going to say 'making love' but that wasn't what they would be doing, yet 'intercourse' sounded too clinical. So he kissed her instead of finishing the sentence, and felt her tense body relax as she kissed him back.

Although the kiss had a far from relaxing effect on his body, and he knew Grace would know it.

They said goodnight at the door, although his hand lingered on her tight, demin-clad butt as she unlocked the door and slipped inside.

How had that Paul let her go?

How had he not read the ripe sensuality of the woman behind the cool, detached image she so carefully projected?

Two things to consider as he drove home—better by far than the dark memories that had come back to haunt him earlier.

Morning, and Grace was once again in a clothes bind. Back to the sensible and classy work clothes, or should she wear one of her new shirts?

She couldn't deny her motivation—she wanted to

look nice for Theo. OK, so their affair might not be the traditional type, begun with excitement and hope and with the possibility of a deeper relationship at the end of it, but that didn't stop her wanting him to want her—even at work.

And the new shirt she was considering was white and as most of her shirts were white, maybe no one would notice she was 'dressing up'!

She pulled it on, doing up the buttons, wondering why one shirt looked neat and another, similar cut and all, looked, well, not sexy but definitely inviting.

Or was she kidding herself?

'Thank heavens, I was about to page you.' Jasmine greeted her as she walked into the small reception area outside the PICU. 'Emergency admission, flown in from the bush. Phil needs you in Theatre ten minutes ago.'

Grace smiled to herself as she ran up the stairs to the next floor, admitting to herself the folly of her morning clothing debate. Theo, if he saw her at all at work today, would be seeing her in theatre garb—all-enveloping gown, cap, goggles and headlamp—really sexy gear!

One of the theatre sisters was in the changing room.

'It's a PDA,' she explained. 'Three-month-old who was doing OK without the ductus arteriosus closing, but suddenly suffering endocarditis in spite of antibiotics. Phil's going to clamp it off using video-assisted thoracoscopic surgery. Have you done much of that? It's so easy on the babies.'

Grace felt a surge of excitement. She'd seen videos of the surgery but had never assisted. The only downside was that with the minimally invasive surgery

Theo wouldn't be present. Although she'd known he was working with Alex today, so why the disappointment?

And why the new shirt?

She wouldn't think about that now.

With no thought beyond that of the child in Theatre in her head, she went through to the scrub room and, once gloved, on into Theatre.

'Done one before?' Phil asked, and she shook her head.

'Piece of cake,' he said, 'always providing we don't puncture the lung. The big thing is to be prepared to open the chest should anything go wrong, but that's never happened with a VAT PDA ligation at Jimmie's—touch wood.'

Grace smiled to herself, wondering what a layperson would think of their casual use of acronyms, although the VAT part was easy—video assisted thorascope—and PDA common enough in hospitals, referring to the tiny tube, the ductus arteriosus that, in a foetus, shuffled blood between the aorta and the pulmonary artery. Shortly after birth this tube closed, but in some babies it remained open—therefore patent, meaning that the blood, which should be flowing into the aorta could take the path of least resistance and flow back into the lungs, causing potential problems for the baby.

She was thinking about this as Phil positioned the unconscious baby the way he wanted him, propped his little form with disposable pads to keep him still, and made four small incisions in his chest.

'Much better than the usual surgical incision,' Grace

murmured, as she watched. 'We're not cutting muscles or bones and we don't have to retract the rib cage, which means far less stress on the baby's body and makes for a far better recovery every time.'

With a mechanical arm holding the videoscope in place, Phil was able to insert forceps into one of the incisions and, with cotton swabs, carefully move the left lobe of the baby's lung out of the way. The videoscope now gave them a perfect view inside the small chest, the vagus and pharyngeal nerves both obvious and possible to avoid. Through another hole Phil used an endoscope to put clips on the little blood vessel, clamping off both ends of it to stop the flow of blood.

'I'm putting a tube in one of the incisions, just until we've reinflated the lung. If there's any damage to the lung we'll know before little Jasper here leaves Theatre and we can use the thoracostomy tube if we need to remove air from his chest cavity.'

Grace glanced at the clock on the far wall. The whole operation had taken less than an hour, and now Jasper was breathing and there was no sign of damage to the left lobe of his lung, the tube could be released. Although he would stay in hospital overnight, where he could be watched for any possible reaction, it was likely he'd be going home the following day. A great result for the little boy, and proof that minimally invasive surgery was gaining ground in their field.

Grace checked the operating list—nothing major, nothing that would require bypass yet a full day nonetheless.

Yes, wearing the new shirt had been stupid.

* * *

'Some days go easy and some days go hard,' Phil said. He was leaning against the wall of the theatre next to the soiled clothes bin but was obviously too weary to strip off even his gloves.

Grace leant on the other side, while between them, Phil's surgical assistant held both their headlamps, the cords trailing on the floor.

'It was as if some gremlin had got into the theatre,' he muttered, staring at the headlamps as if they might hold the answer. 'Everything that could go wrong did.'

'Except the PDA,' Grace reminded the two men. 'That was great. It was only after that things started going berserk.'

Phil grinned at her.

'Going berserk? Can you call it going berserk when a three-year-old having a minor repair for a narrowing of the pulmonary artery arrests on the table?'

'You saved her, she'll be OK,' Grace reminded him, remembering the frantic massaging of the little girl's heart that had got it beating again.

'Yes, but why do these things happen? That's what we need to find out. We're advancing so we can do more and more repairs through keyhole surgery, then we get something like that today and we don't know why.'

Wearily, Phil stripped off his gloves and tossed them in the bin, then followed them with his mask and cap, and finally his gown. He stood there for a moment, a good-looking man in nothing more than boxer shorts, but Grace felt no squirmy feelings deep inside her, or even the faintest glimmer of curiosity.

So what was it about attraction? she wondered as she in turn stripped off her theatre clothes and made her way into the changing room. Why did one male body make the blood heat when others made no impression at all?

It must be different for men, she decided, or girlie magazines wouldn't sell. She'd have to ask Theo later.

The thought brought her up short as she adjusted the water in the shower. First that it seemed so natural that she could talk to Theo about such things, but the second hitch in her thinking was worse. Had they talked about a later? As far as she could remember, they'd made no arrangements to meet again, no doubt assuming they'd see each other at work.

But they hadn't and she felt something that could only be disappointment coiling in her belly.

She could phone him, she decided as water cascaded down her body, dousing her hair and sloshing around her feet while she stood still beneath it and tried to think.

The phoning-him suggestion hadn't done anything to relieve whatever coiled inside her, and she scoffed at the notion that she was too prudish to make such a move. You've asked this man to father a baby for you and you can't phone him? her head mocked, but the coiling stayed and she knew she wouldn't.

'You were so long in there I was going to come in and join you.'

Theo was lounging against the wall of the changing room, still in theatre green, when she emerged from the cubicle, already dressed but with her shirt only partially buttoned and not yet tucked into her skirt.

'How did you know it was me?' she asked, the coiling

turning to heat although she prayed it wasn't yet obvious.

'Shoes!' he said, tapping her shoes—the sensible dancing pumps she invariably wore to work—with his toe. 'Plus the fact that Phil's soap doesn't smell like orange blossom.'

He grinned at her.

'It's nice. I like it.'

She didn't know what to say, but as other members of Alex's team came wandering in, she didn't say anything. As she walked across to slip on her shoes and gather her belongings, Theo touched her lightly on the arm, and spoke quietly so only she could hear.

'Dinner at the brasserie? I'll be ready in ten. You want to go straight from here or go home first? And, no, don't do up that button, it's incredibly sexy.'

Now she knew she'd blush but her fingers, which had been fumbling at the button, trying to find the hole, dropped away.

'I'll wait,' she managed to say, through heat and excitement that she knew was wrong, but couldn't control. How could she possibly want him this much?

'In the PICU?'

He nodded, and headed into the cubicle she'd vacated, pausing in the open doorway and sniffing the still steamy air, then winking at her.

Scarlett seemed a lot better, so much so her mother greeted Grace with a broad smile.

'Dr Attwood says she's improving by the minute, and my mother phoned to say she knows a heart is not far away. My mother's the seventh daughter of a seventh daughter and she has the sight.'

Grace had to smile back. Whatever worked to make Mrs Robinson feel positive was OK with her. In fact, she wondered what Mrs Robinson's mother might see into *her* future…

Stupid!

What was wrong with her?

She read through Scarlett's obs and agreed with Alex that the baby seemed to be improving, which often happened without any intervention or explanation.

'You just hang in there,' she whispered to the tiny girl. 'Your grandma's obviously working on a heart.'

'There *are* other babies in here.'

Theo's voice distracted her and she turned to see him smiling at her—which distracted her a whole lot more.

'I look at all the babies,' she assured him, moving to a crib on the far side of the room. 'And I want to see young Jasper before I leave.'

She thought she was doing really well until Theo touched her in the small of her back, ushering her out of the big room. It was nothing more than a casual gesture of politeness but the skin beneath her shirt burned and excitement fizzed in her blood.

She stopped in the passageway.

'Do we have to have dinner?' she asked, through lips so dry she had to lick them before the words would come out.

'Your place or mine?'

'Yours if that's OK,' she managed. 'Mine…Jean-Luc, Lauren, most of the team live so close.'

Theo nodded, but the desire she could see burning

in his eyes lit fires within her body. She had to take a deep breath and remind herself how important her work was to her, before going into Jasper's room to see the little post-op patient, who was doing well. Phil was also in there and he left the room with her.

'Do you always visit the PICU before you go home?' he asked, and she shook her head.

'Usually I come up later. During the day, the family want to be with their children, but late at night when they've gone off to get what rest they can, I don't feel I'm taking baby time away from them.'

Phil nodded his understanding.

'Theo does the same. He thinks we think he comes to check on those on ECMO but he's a fraud. He loves the little ones as if they were his own—it's as if he empathises with *them* while most of us feel empathy with the parents. Whoops! There he is—early tonight. Hi, Theo, we were just talking about you.'

Theo's questioning eyebrow rose as he looked at Grace, but she'd been so struck by Phil's artless revelations she couldn't think about his eyebrows—or his question—right now. Did Theo really love the babies in their care? And if he did, wouldn't he also want to love a child of his own?

Panic fluttered in her stomach where heat had been only minutes earlier, but she managed to wait until they were in his car, heading for his house, before she asked the question.

'You love those children. Why not one of your own?'

Asked far too curtly—crassly—probably too loudly as well.

He didn't answer, pretending concentration on the

traffic, although it was thick so maybe it wasn't pretence. But as he pulled into the parking space outside his terrace house he turned and when he'd switched off the engine, he put his hands out, palms up, towards her.

'I burnt my hands trying to get my baby out of the car. I couldn't undo the straps holding her in the capsule. I couldn't save her. The agony of the burns, the pain of losing the ability to operate—they were nothing compared to the pain I felt in my heart. No, in my whole body. I ached for the loss of that baby, Grace, and I still do when I think about her. I doubted I would survive it, but I did, but I know for certain that I don't want to go through that again—not ever.'

Grace stared out the window, seeing the house he had put so much energy into doing up—understanding that his DIY project was his way of keeping his ghosts at bay.

What he'd said had reassured her, but her heart was aching for his pain and loss and she didn't want to be feeling things for him—not *before* they'd made love. She was worried enough about what would happen after the act, now here she was getting emotionally involved before it.

'We should have gone to dinner,' he said quietly, and she knew what he meant, but she also knew the sex act could bring release and maybe in some small way a little healing, so she leant across and kissed him on the lips.

'If we get hungry later, surely we can order in?' she whispered, still against his mouth, kissing him until she felt him respond and his hands lifted to her shoulders so he could hold her steady while his kiss grew fiercer and more demanding.

But once inside, ushered up the stairs to a bedroom that held a bed the size of a swimming pool and very little else, all Grace's doubts and inhibitions came clumping down on her head and she looked around, probably too wildly, thinking of escape.

'Stop that!' Theo ordered, coming up behind her and clamping his arms around her, bending his head to kiss her neck where the collar of her shirt left a bit of skin showing. 'Stop thinking at all and give yourself up to sensation. Remember how you felt earlier when the signals between us were so strong it's a wonder the PICU didn't get an R rating.'

And while still nibbling at her neck—delicious thrills stole from there to her thighs, via her nipples— he undid the buttons on her shirt, easing it open so his hands could grasp her breasts which seemed to have grown heavy while her nipples were peaking and rubbing irritably against the lace of her bra.

'Delicious,' he murmured. 'Delectable Grace!'

And though she still felt awkward and not a little afraid, she found herself relaxing back against him, trying to ignore the sensations his hands were causing as they ran lightly back and forth across her breasts.

Theo held the woman who'd inadvertently—surely not deliberately—plunged him back into a black mood and, holding her, he found himself relaxing, though not totally relaxing, for sexual excitement was building, hard and hot, so he had to remind himself of her previous bad experience, swearing to himself this would be better for her—that he would think of her first...

'Can we go to bed?' she whispered, pressing back

against him. The hardness and heat intensified to the extent he all but forgot the 'think of her first' scenario.

Turning her, he stripped off her shirt, then her bra, and, seeing the full orbs of her breasts, the nipples pale pink and peaked enticingly he forgot about it altogether and suckled first one breast then the other, murmuring about their beauty, his hands holding her still, although she squirmed and bucked in reaction to his attention.

Finally she grabbed his head and pushed him away, no words spoken as they both stripped off their clothes and, locked together in their first naked kiss, collapsed onto the bed.

She was beautiful. Full and firm, not just her breasts, but all over, her tummy slightly rounded, her hips beautifully fleshed, her legs, her thighs…

'You are so beautiful.'

He *had* to tell her—he couldn't keep his observations to himself—and then he watched as she coloured deliciously, the blush rising from her upper chest to dust her cheeks with dusky rose colour.

Did he mean it or was he just saying it? Grace decided she didn't care. She *felt* beautiful, and not only because of Theo's words but because of the way he was touching her, loving her with his fingers and his lips. She wanted, so badly, to love him in the same way, wanted to touch him and learn about him through the touch of her fingers and her lips, but she was too shy.

Repressed!

The hateful word came back to her—a word Paul had spat at her one day—then as if he'd felt her mood change, Theo was kissing her again, murmuring about her beauty, urging her to touch him as he touched her, and slowly, tentatively, she ran her hands across his skin, surprised to find how satiny the texture was, how smooth, how satisfying just to touch.

'Try lower,' he whispered, and as his hand slid between her thighs and his fingers brushed lightly against her sensitive nub, she reached for him and found him hard and ready, and suddenly she wanted him, right here and now, her desire so intense she was shaking.

'Please, Theo!' She was begging and he heard it, for although he protested that he'd wanted to take it slowly—for their first time together to be special—he slid his fingers into her and must have felt her readiness, moving so he lay between her legs, rising above her, then sliding into her, both of them releasing huge sighs of what sounded like relief before the rhythm of lovemaking took hold of them and they were lost in the momentum that grew and grew until she gave a gasp of pure surprise and was lifted high above the world into a place she'd never been before.

She was vaguely aware of Theo's groan of release, then he slumped on top of her and she held him tightly, wanting his weight to anchor her, to return her to the bed—to life!

# CHAPTER SIX

SHE stayed the night although even as she drifted off to sleep, after making love a second and even more satisfying time, she knew she should go back to her flat. Otherwise she'd have to wake up early in the morning, get a cab home so she could change for work. She wouldn't want to wake Theo to ask him to take her because theirs was a practical arrangement and he was already doing so much for her in helping her get pregnant. Or he would be, she hoped, eventually!

Not to mention showing her how pleasurable making love could be.

She sighed. They'd used protection but, remembering the obvious agony Theo still felt over the loss of his daughter, should she really be expecting him to help her have a child?

Could a man who felt so deeply *not* get emotionally involved with his own child?

Was she asking too much of him?

She sighed again and discarded difficult thoughts, remembering pleasure instead, snuggling up against his warm body, glad he was deeply asleep so he wouldn't realise how feeble she was being, needing reassurance from the closeness of his body.

'Coffee, sleeping beauty!'

He was standing over her, fully dressed but no less gorgeous for the fact he had clothes on.

She tried to regrow her brain, which had apparently dwindled into nothingness overnight. Checking her watch seemed like a good idea—it would stop her staring at him, and probably smiling stupidly!

'Oh, Theo, look at the time.' Now she was wailing—her brain had certainly disappeared. 'I'll never get home in time to change—I'll be late for work. Oh, Theo!'

He grinned at her.

'And to think I thought I'd never see you flustered,' he said, then he leant forward and kissed her on the lips.

Quickly she backed away, putting her hand to her mouth.

'Don't! I must have dragon breath.' But although she'd protested, she was inordinately pleased by the gesture—which was more proof that she'd lost her brain.

Now he sat down on the bed beside her.

'Sweet breath,' he said. 'Now, drink your coffee. I've raisin toast or croissants downstairs if that will do you for breakfast, and if you look in the bathroom you'll find a pristine pair of my jockey shorts, still in the packet.'

His grin widened.

'Think of the fun I'll have all day, imagining you in my undies!'

'But I'll still have to wear the clothes I wore yesterday—what will people think?'

This smile was different. It was kind and gentle and so sweet she wanted to kiss him—only she now knew just how dangerous kissing Theo could be.

'You wear a coat over your clothes so, really, who will notice?' He paused, the smile giving way to an intent look she couldn't really read. 'And if they did, would it matter?'

She stared at him, aware she hadn't thought this through. She'd just spent the night with another member of the team. She wanted to keep seeing this man, and she wasn't entirely sure it was anything to do with procreation. No, that was wrong, wanting to see him again had *nothing* to do with procreation. Although she did want a baby, she just had to think more about Theo's side of things.

The thoughts jumbled through the space in her head where her brain had been, pushing at each other, leaving her so confused she lifted the cup of coffee and brought it to her lips.

'No one's ever brought me coffee in bed before.'

Duh! What a stupid thing to say!

Now doubly embarrassed—by this admission as well as by the intimacy that seemed to have developed between them—she gulped down the rapidly cooling liquid.

'I'd better have a shower,' she added, as she replaced the cup on its saucer, then she realised she was sitting up in his bed, stark naked, and would be even more naked, somehow, as she made her way to the bathroom.

Theo must have seen her concern for he leaned over and kissed her once again.

'Coffee breath now, and you're beautiful. You should never feel shame about being naked in front of me, or any man.'

He'd added the last bit because she was so darned insecure, but as he said it Theo felt a definite twinge of what could only be jealousy. This might be a 'no emotional attachment' type of relationship but he certainly didn't want her parading around naked in front of any other men. In fact, he was probably going to have to talk to her about coming out of the shower cubicle in bra and panties when male members of the team were about.

Only there was no way he could say something like that! And now he thought about it, he'd only once seen her come out of the cubicle not dressed and that had been the day all the cubicles had been full and he'd yelled out for someone to hurry and she'd come out to let him use the one she'd been in.

And when she'd emerged she'd been clutching all her clothes in front of her so it wasn't until he'd come out he'd seen her in the bra and panties.

And lusted just a little…

He watched her scurry to the bathroom, and knew she was trying not to scurry—trying hard to walk calmly and nonchalantly—but her feet kept hurrying her anyway.

She was so beautiful naked he wanted to be naked with her again, but if he walked into that bathroom they'd never get to work—well, not on time.

'You realise,' he said as he drove to work, from time to time sneaking a look at the slight smile of satisfaction still lingering on Grace's face, 'that even without the fact that some of the women might realise you're wearing yesterday's clothes, the people we work with will soon realise we're having an affair.'

She turned to him with the perplexed look that always made him realise just how fragile her façade of cool sophistication was.

'How?' she asked, and he laughed out loud.

'One look at your face and Becky, who runs gossip central in the unit, will know you've had satisfying sex.'

He paused, suddenly doubtful.

'It *was* satisfying, wasn't it?'

Had she read his uncertainty that she touched him lightly on the forearm?

'Very satisfactory,' she murmured, colour rising delicately pink in her cheeks. 'And I don't think it will hurt me to have people knowing, but you? They know you better. In fact, they know you well enough for someone to tell me that you don't get involved with other members of the team, so there'll be talk about you making an exception. And then you'll be here when I've gone—it will be worse for you.'

The colour had disappeared from her cheeks and she was looking genuinely worried.

For him?

It seemed so, and although he hadn't liked how he'd felt when she'd pressed home the point that she'd be gone, he spoke quickly, reassuring her it was none of anyone else's business and while they might talk among themselves it was unlikely anyone would say anything to either of them directly.

'Which just goes to show how little you know!' Grace muttered to herself as she made her way to Phil's consulting room, after Becky, the unit secretary, had greeted her with a beaming smile and an innocent-sounding 'Nice night?' question.

But it *had* been a nice night. More than nice, in fact, and though she'd grown back enough brain to cope very coolly and efficiently with all the consultations she was taking for Phil while he gave a paper at a conference in Melbourne, deep inside she could still feel echoes of the sheer delight that had transported her to places far, far away.

Grace galaxy?

The consultations went well, three children to be booked for operations later on, four follow-up cases and finally an older patient, sixteen-year-old Kelly Groves—no case file, just a note from Becky to say she was a last-minute appointment.

Kelly came into the room on her own—well, a sixteen-year-old didn't need her parents with her—but one look at her, at her rounded, slightly puffy face, suggested to Grace that the teenager was on anti-rejection drugs.

'You wanted to see Dr Park. I'm afraid he's not in, but can I help you?' Grace offered as Kelly sat down, clasping her shiny pink handbag in her lap.

'Probably not, but I doubt if Dr Park could either.' Kelly paused then gave an embarrassed half-shrug. 'I kind of told a lie to the secretary so I could get an appointment. I told her Dr Park had operated on me at another hospital when I was a baby and that I was visiting someone in the hospital so I thought I might say hello to him and thank him. The thing is, I keep wanting to know and I thought Dr Park, or even you perhaps, might be able to help me to go on without knowing.'

Grace listened to the words and wondered if she'd lost her brain again for they didn't seem to be making much sense. But the young woman was obviously agitated so Grace prompted her.

'Knowing?' she said gently.

'Knowing who has my heart.'

The words burst from Kelly's lips, making even less sense than the lead-up conversation had. The girl was very much alive so she must have a heart.

'Your heart?'

Kelly smiled.

'Isn't it weird?' she said. 'Wouldn't you, like, want to know, if it was you? I know it's all about confidentiality but I feel—I want to know if my heart's working for whoever got it, like if he or she is OK, and I wondered if I could just find out that much.'

Grace stared at the girl. She had to have a heart or she wouldn't be there.

Light dawned.

'You had a heart-lung transplant and your heart went to someone else? Cystic fibrosis?'

Kelly nodded.

'It's a year ago and I'm fine but now I know *I'm* OK I can't stop thinking about the other person. At night I dream about her—to me it's a her because I can't imagine my heart in a teenage boy. I mean, how would he feel—would he have girl feelings in his heart instead of boy feelings?'

Grace wanted to assure Kelly that hearts didn't really feel emotions but something in her chest had ached when Paul had jilted her.

Still, she had to try…

'You know other civilisations believe other organs are the seat of our emotions—some think the kidneys, or the liver—but, really, what we feel comes from what we think so I don't think a boy with a girl's heart would feel anything other than tremendously grateful to the girl who gave it to him. You already know about the confidentiality of organ donor lists and, yes, it must be hard for you not to know, but Phil—Dr Park—couldn't tell you who got your heart any more than the donor centre can. I've only been here a short time, but I know from the records I read before coming that Phil hasn't lost a patient in the last year, so we can assume your heart is going well and doing a great job for someone. Does that help?'

She watched Kelly think about it, but she was obviously more interested in the first part of the conversation than in the health of her heart recipient.

'You mean you have to think about things—love and stuff—with your head before you feel it in your body?'

Grace wasn't entirely certain this was true. The attraction between her and Theo was so strong—on her part anyway—she all but lost her head whenever he was near.

'I think physical attraction doesn't need much thinking about,' she admitted. 'You know, getting goosebumps when you're near a boy you like.' Did teenagers get goose-bumps? 'But real love, the kind that might hurt your heart, or your liver in another civilisation, well, that has more to do with your head than your body.'

Good grief! Was she really spouting this rubbish? Did she believe it? She had no idea, but Kelly seemed to be thinking about her words so they might be helping.

'But what about babies?'

This question came out of the blue, fitting into Grace's mindset in a positively creepy way.

'Babies?'

'If it's a boy with my heart, will he love his babies like a man or like a woman?'

Grace smiled.

'I think men and women love their babies in the same way. I think both their hearts hurt when their babies cry.'

Theo's wouldn't because he wouldn't hear their baby cry. She *had* to think about this!

'But it's not really their heart that's hurting, it's emotion causing their distress,' she added, 'and emotion can change the way we breathe and the way our hearts work, so we might experience a dull ache in the chest and we say it's heartache but really it's a physical manifestation of the change in our bodies because of the emotion we're feeling.'

Once again the young woman with the most unusual reason for visiting a specialist Grace had ever heard seemed to be thinking.

'I think I understand,' she finally said. 'Mind you, if he or she is anything like me, when I get a pain in the chest I panic and think something's gone wrong medically, not that I might be suffering love heartache.'

'That's a sensible way to feel, although you seem extremely healthy. Your specialists are happy with your progress?'

Kelly beamed.

'Very happy,' she said. 'It's a year ago today and look at me.'

She stood up and twirled around, her skirt flying out around her legs.

'Before I would have been breathless standing up and I certainly couldn't have turned around.'

'Then you must be extremely grateful to the person whose heart and lungs you received and you should understand that whoever got your heart is feeling just as grateful to you.'

'But it's different for me,' Kelly argued. 'Because my donor is dead and though I'm grateful to his or her family for donating the organs, I don't have to worry about what's happening in his or her life, if you know what I mean!'

Grace did, but Kelly obviously had more to say so she waited.

'The thing is, it's horrid having to go on being grateful—I know, because I've been sick all my life that I can remember, and people were always doing nice things for me and my family, and we went on trips and had camps and I liked all that but you have to keep thanking people and it kind of bugs you after a while, and what I really wanted to say to my heart person is that there's no need to feel grateful to me, because I only gave him or her something that would have been tossed in the rubbish otherwise.'

A heart tossed in the rubbish—the analogy was too close for comfort as far as Grace was concerned but Kelly was talking about real hearts, not emotion, except that gratitude was an emotion.

'I don't think you should worry about the person

being grateful,' Grace said, 'because telling someone not to be grateful isn't going to stop them. Your person might not think about you every day, but I'm sure when something nice happens in his or her life, like a beautiful sunny day after rain, or seeing a really good football game if it's a boy, then I'm sure somewhere inside they say thank you to you, sending out a message into the ether and probably hoping that just as nice things are happening to you.'

Once again Kelly seemed to consider the words, then she smiled.

'I reckon I can live with that,' she said, 'so that will do for emotion, but what about practical stuff? What if my heart went to a boy and I meet him in ten years' time and we fall in love—would that be OK for our babies and stuff?'

Grace smiled at her.

'Do you lie awake at night thinking up difficult questions for doctors to answer?'

Kelly returned her smile.

'No, I lie awake at night listening to my lungs work—or not listening to them. But would babies be OK?'

'Babies would be OK,' Grace assured her, 'but as two people with complex medical issues in your pasts, you'd need to have genetic testing because your babies could inherit the problems you both had. And you'd probably have to go into enough detail about your medical conditions that the chances are you'd find out he had your heart.'

'Wow! Wouldn't that be great?'

Bizarre would be closer to the mark, Grace thought,

but she didn't say it. Teenage girls should be allowed to keep their dreams.

She walked out with Kelly, said goodbye to her at the front desk, and was heading back to the consultation room to tidy up the files and dictate a note to Phil when Becky stopped her.

'She wasn't really one of Phil's old babies, was she?' she asked.

Seventh daughter of a seventh daughter?

'What makes you think that?' Grace asked, dismissing the irreverent thought.

'Phil grew up in England, he became a surgeon there, not here, and Kelly didn't have an English accent.'

'Of course,' Grace said, then she had to ask. 'But if you knew that, why did you make an appointment for her?'

Becky shrugged.

'To be truthful, it was because you were there. If Phil had been here I would have told her he had no time available, made an appointment in a month or two to keep her happy, then talked to Phil. But she seemed, I don't know, uptight somehow, and she was on medication from the look of her, so I didn't really want to upset her. Besides which, Phil is great and terrific with patients but I didn't know how much empathy he'd have with teenage girls.'

Grace digested this information then once again had to ask.

'And what made you think I would?'

Becky beamed at her.

'You come across all cool and calm and collected,

but I reckon you've got a heart as big as South Africa. Is South Africa bigger or smaller than Australia? I don't know much about it except for wild animals.'

The talk had veered from country sizes into zebras, which apparently were Becky's favourite animal, then drifted away as idle conversation did until Grace said she had to dictate her notes and Becky remembered she had a fitting for her wedding dress and they parted, Becky apparently oblivious to the fact that she'd shocked Grace to her core.

A big heart?

Did Becky know about the arrangement she'd made for the Robinsons to come to Sydney? Grace had worked so hard to keep the donation anonymous and it had been practicality, not sentiment, that had prompted her to see the hospital social worker to find out how she could help get them closer to their baby. All it had needed had been some money—practical stuff!

She'd always considered her heart more detached than anything else…

But as she dictated the notes for Phil, she pondered how often hearts had cropped up in her day then mocked herself because that was what she did—fixed hearts.

But the conversation she'd had with Kelly remained with her, and though she knew full well the heart wasn't the seat of the emotions, hers still skipped a beat when she bumped into Theo in the tearoom.

Unfortunately, another part of Kelly's conversation popped up in her head—the part about gratitude— and she suddenly felt uneasy in her lover's presence. Not that there was anything lover-like in his attitude and she hoped, in front of several members of the team, she was behaving equally coolly. But gratitude stuck with her, so when, later, they did walk down the road to the brasserie, she had to speak to him about it.

'I talked to someone today about gratitude,' she began, cautious at first because for all they'd spent the night together she felt they didn't know each other very well, and she was feeling shy and awkward once again. But once she'd begun the words came tumbling out. 'And it made me realise that you're doing me this big favour and, of course, I'm grateful but I'd like to think you're getting something out of it as well, so I don't have to keep on being overly grateful, if you know what I mean.'

Theo gave a shout of laughter and pulled her into his arms—right outside Scoozi where, no doubt, half the hospital was having dinner.

'Oh, Grace,' he said, giving her a hug then swinging her around so they were all but dancing on the sidewalk. 'You really are the world's most insecure woman. For a start, at this stage there's no great favour being done— we're using protection, remember. And on top of that, do you think I was putting on my enjoyment last night? Do you think I wouldn't have stuck with a non-physical union if you'd repelled me? Not, as I said, that any major decision has been taken yet.'

He let her go but only to drag her into the shadow of a tree, so he could look down into her face.

Not only look at her, but punctuate his words with kisses.

'You—' kiss '—are—' kiss '—one—' kiss '—sexy—' kiss '—delicious—' kiss '—delectable—' kiss '—woman.' kiss.

Then he straightened up, put his hands on her shoulders and looked into her eyes, his own saying things that made her shiver.

'Understand?'

She managed a nod, although she was beginning to think she could easily go without dinner again tonight...

They did eat dinner at the brasserie, not only that night but many other nights, varying their diet by trying some of the many restaurants closer to Theo's home, one night eating fish and chips on a beach close by. But every night ended up in the same way, together in Theo's big bed, until it became difficult for Grace to remember just why they were doing this.

Until she realised that six weeks had gone by. The food they'd shopped for back when she'd first arrived had long since been moved to Theo's place or thrown out, most of her clothes were now hung in his dressing room, and the little flat in Kensington Terrace was nothing more than a memory.

Six weeks!

She hadn't had a period!

But they were still using protection, weren't they?

She tried to think back to any time they might have been careless but her brain had gone missing again, although this time it was because her head had filled with panic. Theo had said he'd wanted to get to know her better before she tried to conceive, but as she'd grown to know him better, she'd realised it was because he was wary of having another child—the pain of Elena's loss still too deep.

And right now, she realised, Theo's feelings were more important than her desire to have a child.

In fact, now that she considered it, Theo was more important to her than any child.

Oh, dear, had she fallen in love?

How could that have happened? It wasn't what she wanted at all and it *definitely* wasn't what Theo wanted!

Not that Theo need know.

Too confused to think about love, she thought about her body, wondering if she could feel any changes in it.

As if!

But it was a Saturday morning. She was off duty but Theo was working. She had intended taking a bus to the city and have a look around, something she'd done with Theo, but then they'd done tourist things—the Opera House, The Rocks. This time she'd thought she'd look around the shops.

What she should now do was find a pharmacy…

It was ridiculous—they'd been using protection…

'And if you are?'

She asked herself the question out loud because she knew it was important.

If she *was* pregnant then she'd have no excuse to keep up the relationship with Theo. Her goal would have been achieved.

But at the cost of losing Theo?

And although she assured herself a hundred times a day that she was *not* getting emotionally involved with him, she didn't want to end their affair—not just yet…

What a muddle. The thought of shifting out of Theo's house—out of his bed—was so upsetting she was almost tempted to not get a test. She could ignore the fact she was late and just go on as before.

Or do a test, find out, but not tell Theo.

That option made her feel sick and very, very ashamed that she could even consider such deception.

Getting out of bed was a start. She *would* go into the city. She *would* buy a test kit.

She dressed but then, instead of catching one of the buses she knew ran along the adjoining street every ten minutes, she caught a cab, asking the driver to drop her at the Queen Victoria Building, the only landmark she knew right in the centre of Sydney. Somewhere nearby she'd find a pharmacy.

Which all worked well, but having the test kit was suddenly not enough—she had to know and she had to know now! A public toilet in a big department store was hardly the best place to find out if her long-term dream had been fulfilled, but that's exactly where she did find out that the baby she so desperately wanted was already growing inside her.

She stared at the line on the stick, checked the packet's instructions to make sure she was reading it properly, checked the line again then gave a whoop of joy.

She *was* pregnant! It had happened!

She couldn't stop smiling. To have a baby—to have a child on whom she could lavish a mother's love, the love she'd missed out on as a child. Yes, her father had been wonderful, but she knew instinctively a mother's love was different.

Necessary!

Coffee to celebrate?

Hell, no, she'd have to give up coffee.

This early, would it matter?

She had no idea but decided she'd become a weak-tea drinker.

And that being the case, there was no way she could *not* tell Theo! As if he wouldn't guess, when she who was a coffee addict suddenly took to weak tea...

Theo!

How could she have been so excited when she felt, deep in her heart, Theo really didn't want another child?

Although now they knew each other better, might things not work out?

Might she not be able to have Theo *and* a child?

He'd already spoken, occasionally, of visiting South Africa—maybe even working there some time. Good perfusionists could get work anywhere in the world...

But the excitement she'd felt when she'd first seen the confirmation failed to return. She may have fallen in love with Theo but in no way had he indicated he had similar feelings for her...

At least she'd have his child...

Theo knew he shouldn't be feeling excitement at the simple fact of coming home from work and knowing Grace would be waiting for him, but it was the first time their days off hadn't coincided and there had been something different about going off to work while she had been lazing in the bed—so warm and inviting he'd been tempted to be late—and now, coming home to her, was even more— It couldn't be exciting, their relationship being the way it was…

He smelt the aromas as soon as he walked in.

Grace cooking?

She'd told him she was a hopeless cook and had insisted on paying for dinner on the nights they went out, which, as she kept claiming, were the nights it was her turn to cook.

But something was definitely sizzling in the kitchen, or perhaps on the barbeque, and whatever it was smelled delicious.

But no more delicious than the woman who came running lightly down the steps to greet him as he closed the door.

She was wearing the tight jeans that had his libido stirring just thinking about them, and his hands itching to strip them off her when he saw her in them. But no white shirt. No, tonight she was in a pale blue-aqua T-shirt, the same colour as her eyes, so tight it clung to the breasts she said were too big.

'Been shopping?' he asked, super-casual, hoping his desire for her wasn't throbbing in his voice the way it was throbbing in his body.

'I have indeed,' she said, smiling at him and coming into his open arms, wrapping hers around him so they stood, their bodies pressed together, remembering…

'And not only for T-shirts,' she teased, kissing his neck and nibbling on his earlobe. 'I shopped for food. We're eating in—my treat.'

'We should have different days off more often,' he murmured, pressing his lips against her cheek. Then he remembered the days off they'd shared, rarely leaving the bed, and added, 'Or maybe not.'

His hands moved to the button on her jeans, wanting her, ready for her, wanting her now.

Her hands stopped his.

'No way—we're eating first,' she said, then she kissed him lightly on the lips.

Was it just the day's separation that had made her so…? Teasing was the only word he could come up with, but Grace never teased and didn't handle being teased all that well, although *he* teased her all the time and she was getting better at handling it.

And sexually she could tease—oh, could she tease! He shook his head in wonder at the sexually liberated woman who now shared his bed—at the change their relationship had brought to her, from their first tentative kiss when she'd haltingly apologised for her inadequacy as a lover.

He felt anger burn deep inside him as it always did when he thought of the rat who'd hurt her so badly and of the damage it had done to her. Damage only he, most probably, would ever know or see…

Unless, of course, she married someone else back in South Africa.

The thought came out of nowhere, but now it was there, it horrified him. She wouldn't! She couldn't!

Of course she could—she was beautiful, more beautiful than when he'd first seen her, the sexual confidence that had been lacking somehow giving her an inner glow.

What man wouldn't want her?

His gut knotted at the thought but she'd already disappeared into the kitchen and as he'd been as adamant as she that this was nothing more than an affair, he could hardly change the rules now.

# CHAPTER SEVEN

'IT's a braaivleis—an Afrikaans barbeque,' she explained. 'I couldn't believe it when I saw the sausages in the wonderful food hall of a big department store. I knew I had to get some for you, then phone Margie in the middle of the night to ask her how to make mieliepap to go with them and the gravy—I really can't cook.'

He'd followed her as far as the kitchen before she turned and he saw once again the uncertainty that lay beneath her composed exterior.

'I know the sausages—we call them boerewors— might be a bit spicy for your taste. They have thyme and nutmeg and coriander and allspice and cloves and—'

He stopped her with a kiss.

'Whatever you cook for me will taste delicious,' he whispered. 'And even if the food is not to my taste, I know the afters will be just fine.'

His kiss intensified and he wondered if the food would spoil if they had just a quick...

But then he realised she wasn't with him in the kiss—not responding with the heat and joy she usually gave back to him.

Of course, she was worried about the meal—the first she'd cooked for him. He stopped kissing her and asked what wine they should open to have with it.

'Red would be best but just a very small glass for me,' she said.

Definitely anxious about the cooking!

He carried the wine and glasses into the courtyard where the table was already set and the barbeque lit. Grace was stirring something in a pot on one side of the barbeque, the strange sausages already grilling on the other side, giving off tantalisingly tempting aromas.

'We could have had them with salad but I went traditional. There's a salad in the refrigerator if you really don't like the miclicpap and there are regular sausages in there as well.'

Theo carried his glass of wine over to the barbeque.

'Will you stop with the negativity? The dinner will be fine—the sausages smell delicious. For someone who is so good at what they do, not to mention so beautiful, you are unbelievably insecure. You have to start believing in yourself. You have to think, if Theo doesn't like my— What did you call them?'

'Boerewors,' she said, a little smile playing about her lips.

'Right, boerewors. If Theo doesn't like them, he can starve.'

'But then you mightn't be any good in bed later,' she said, the smile broadening, and he stared at her in disbelief.

'You teased me!'

And, forgetful of the grill and pots and pans, he put his arms around her from behind and kissed her neck.

'You're learning! Oh, Grace, you are one wonderful woman!'

He had to let her go so she could turn the sausages, and realising she was getting tense he left her to her cooking. He sat down at the table, sipping at his wine, watching her concentration and her movements, thinking how good things were—how satisfying—suspecting for a minute that he might actually be happy.

'That was extraordinarily good,' he said, some time later, sitting back and looking at the woman across the table who was positively glowing with delight at her achievements.

'I'm not sure I got the mieliepap right but it didn't taste too bad, did it?'

He shook his head, seeing once again the insecurity which he'd thought their being together had laid to rest.

'Not only worked but possibly filled me up so much I might not be able to move, let alone make love to you.'

She smiled, the half shy, half teasing smile that stirred him deep inside, and said, 'Then don't move. Let's sit and talk.'

Was it a measure of how well he felt his life was going that no warning bells clanged in his head?

But, then, why *would* such innocent words set off alarms?

'So talk,' he said, relaxing back in his chair, sipping the coffee she'd made. 'Or do you want a rundown on my day? Scarlett is still doing well. It's funny because I know she's far too young and too sedated to know whether her parents are by her side or not but she seems to have done better since they were there. Whoever organised that was a miracle worker. Alex's ops went well, although at one stage a coronary artery bled and there was a panic.'

He smiled across the table, where Grace was leaning back against the wall of the house, nodding at him, a little smile on her lips but a glow in her eyes that urged him to finish his coffee and be done with talk.

'Now your turn,' he said. 'You've obviously been out. I love the T-shirt and it's rubbish that you shouldn't wear fitted shirts. You look sensational.'

She didn't respond but, then, she rarely did, somehow embarrassed by any compliments he paid her—certainly, he was sure, to do with not having had a mother telling her she was pretty as she'd grown up.

'I did shop,' she confirmed, not smiling now—in fact, looking rather tense and anxious. 'Not only for clothes and food but for one other thing. I know it was stupid but I was late…'

She was obviously too stressed to go on, but why?

He reran the conversation through his head.

Late?

What on earth could she be talking about?

'I'm usually very regular so I bought a pregnancy testing kit. It was awful testing in the public toilet in the shop but once I had it I had to know and—it showed positive. I'm pregnant. Theo, I know you didn't want it to happen yet, but I did want a baby and now I have you to thank for it and I'm so grateful I don't know how to thank you.'

Theo could only stare at her, so stunned by this—not by the news that she was pregnant but by the implications of it—he couldn't speak.

What was he supposed to feel?

Not angry, he was sure, but it was definitely anger simmering inside him.

'You're pregnant?' he heard the anger say. 'We used protection. Or did you do this deliberately? Stick pins in the condoms? Sabotage them in some way?'

The light in the courtyard wasn't bright, but it was still bright enough for him to see the colour leave her cheeks.

'I can't believe you'd think that of me!'

But beneath the quiet words he heard all the old Grace-uncertainty return and cursed himself, but couldn't control his rage.

'What am I supposed to think?' he demanded. 'You've certainly got what you want, you can't deny that.'

'I'll move out now, if that's what you want,' she said, so quietly he once again had to repeat the words in his head to make sense of them.

'Of course it's not what I want!' he muttered—then congratulated himself. Surely he'd got that bit right.

But apparently not entirely right.

'You don't sound too certain,' she said, standing up and picking up their plates, hovering over the table, waiting…

'How can I be when you spring this on me?' he growled, standing up himself and picking up the salt and pepper mills. 'I don't know what to think!'

The glow had faded from her eyes, which now looked lost and haunted, and once again he was struck by just how insecure this woman was.

And how much that insecurity hurt him!

He shouldn't be holding salt and pepper mills, he should be holding her, he knew that, but he didn't free his hands, instead following her inside. The two of them were as awkward as they'd been when first they had met—when everything they had said to each other had seemed to come out wrongly.

He set the mills down on the counter in the kitchen and turned to where she was rinsing their plates at the sink. He put his arms around her and held her against his body, knowing he had to make things right between them but not sure how.

'Congratulations—you're going to be a mum!'

He squeezed her gently, still trying to get his thoughts into some kind of rational order, still aware something was missing from this conversation.

He tried again.

'And your father will have his grandchild. You'll have to find an obstetrician—you want to be seeing someone good while you're in Australia. And you may as well stay here, because we do enjoy each other's company—don't we? And just think, if you get the dreaded morning sickness, I'll be around to hold your hand.'

Grace didn't need to replay the conversation in her head to know she was disappointed in his reaction, though why she didn't know.

Or, more likely, she knew but didn't want to consider it. It all went back to his initial accusation—that she'd done this deliberately in spite of his precautions. The hurt of it was like a bruise deep inside her, one that would be there for a long time.

But what to do right now?

She had no idea.

In fairness she had to give Theo time to get used to the idea of a baby. He didn't want a child at all but maybe…

No, she was being foolish. There was no maybe.

But as she stood there, wasting water while he held her from behind, touching her breasts and belly and wondering how soon they'd change, she felt…bereft. She'd stupidly wanted Theo to share her joy, but of course he wouldn't—couldn't…

'Right, out of the kitchen with you. The cook never washes up. Leave me to clean up and stack the dishwasher. You take your tiny, tiny foetus and go to bed.'

She went, but in the shower she wept, knowing that the one thing she'd dreaded had indeed occurred. Making love with Theo, living with him so she saw him day and night, learning little things about him, growing dependent on his strength of character, she'd gone and got herself so emotionally involved with him it had to be love.

Which *was*, of course, her problem, not his—and he must never know.

She dried her eyes and then her body, and when he came to bed, his naked body joining hers, literally, beneath the sheets, she shut her stupidity out of her mind and enjoyed the bliss of being Theo's lover.

The next day, Sunday, they were both off duty, and Grace lay in bed beside Theo, relaxed and almost happy. They were reading Sunday papers, sharing little bits of news or snippets of interest, life going on as it had before the little strip on the stick had told her she was pregnant.

Although not quite the same. She'd changed, she knew that. No matter that the secret of her feelings for him were tucked away inside her, the very fact she had the secret made her feel different—less at ease.

And Theo, too, had changed. He'd not said much but she could feel it, and feeling it wondered if he *did* want her to move out.

Not that she could broach the subject—she didn't dare to. The one thing she *had* decided, there beneath the shower, had been that she wanted to spend as much time as possible with him, to gather together a good store of memories to take with her, not only when she went but to hold to her heart through the rest of her life.

'I'll phone a gynaecologist I know at the hospital, he'll tell me who's the best OB man for you to go to. We want to see you get the best care from the beginning.'

The statement came out of the blue and when Grace dropped her paper from in front of her face to look at Theo, she realised he'd folded his newspaper and set it down on the bedside table and was staring towards the window, wearing his 'thinking' face.

'That's terrific of you to bother but I don't think obstetricians want to see any patients until they're at least a couple of months gone.'

'It's not terrific of me, it's my baby too,' he said, still contemplating the window, which showed nothing but an expanse of blue sky. 'I do have some responsibility.'

Then he turned to her.

'Do you know at what gestation stage they do the scans that show the sex? I'm thinking a boy would be best. Not that it matters, but for business I think it would be less stressful for a man to manage business than a woman who might want to be juggling family and a career already.'

Grace stared at him, trying desperately to make sense of what he was saying.

'What *are* you talking about?'

'The baby. Best if it's a boy, although of course we can't do anything about it now.'

He'd turned towards her and offered this second statement with the air of a man who'd made everything crystal clear.

'Theo!' Grace said, exasperation making the word far too loud. 'What do you mean? Why should it matter?'

He smiled at her and she had to push away the emotional involvement problem very forcefully because Theo's smiles made her so warm and happy it was no wonder she'd become emotionally involved.

'The baby.'

'What about the baby? Why better if it's a boy? Is this purely male chauvinism or what?'

Theo shook his head and hitched himself back against the pillows, folding his arms across his naked chest.

'No, I've been thinking about it, and it's not all bad. Although I know females probably have more nous than males, I think because men usually have a woman backing them up, they are better able to handle major responsibilities.'

It still made no sense to Grace.

'Theo, this child, male or female, might be a chef, or a librarian, or a waitress or a labourer. Whatever he or she decides to do, I'll back it, and there'll be no worries financially because he or she will inherit my money and my father's and there'll be enough there to set him or her up. But although there'll be money, there's not so much it would make for a major responsibility.'

'Except for my money,' he said.

'*You've* got money?'

Grace hoped she didn't sound as startled as she felt, but she couldn't help looking around. Yes, Theo had made the little terrace house very snug but it hardly shouted major-responsibility-type wealth.

'Quite a lot,' he said, almost apologetically. 'Though the bigger part of it is tied up in a trust for my child or children. My father died when I was still married but as he didn't like or trust my wife, he left the major portion of his money to my issue. After the accident, as I had no intention of having more children, I'd resigned myself to it going to some fairly worthless cousins who've already gone through the money their father left to them. But then, when you started talking about the baby, I realised it was the perfect solution. Of course, because it's quite a lot of money, I'll probably have to be more involved in the child's upbringing than you'd perhaps like, but to take on my father's legacy, the child will need some special training in financial matters.'

Theo thought he was explaining things rather well, but apparently something had upset Grace for she was out of bed, staring down at him with much the same expression he thought he would be wearing when faced with a man-eating alligator.

'You want this baby so it can inherit your father's

money? You had this ulterior motive all along and didn't think to mention it to me? And you accuse *me* of sticking pins in your bloody condoms! Oh, no, it was all Theo doing a big favour for Grace—getting the little woman pregnant—when all along you were conniving behind my back, plotting, planning. Did you never pause to think I might like to know these things? Did it never occur to you that I might not want my child to have some great inheritance hanging over his or her head?'

'But how could you not want your own child to be wealthy?'

He thought it was a valid question but all he got was a scoffing laugh.

'You don't get it, do you?' she said, now pulling on clothes as fast as she could, picking them up from the tangle on the floor where they'd hastily discarded them last night. 'It's not only the wealth, it's the secrecy thing. Here I'm thinking you're doing this for me, and I'm under obligation to you, to say nothing of feeling gratitude, when all along you've had your own agenda. One you didn't even consider sharing with me. How's that for trust? I've been open and honest with you from the start, Theo Corones, and you've deceived me.'

And on that note she stormed out of the bedroom, and out of the house minutes later, because he heard the front door slam.

He stayed in bed, running the conversation back and forth in his head, wondering where he'd gone so wrong. Unfortunately, it all sounded quite rational to him so he put it down to Grace's hormones being out of kilter, decided she would go back to the flat and he'd give her time to calm down then call her later. After all, most of her clothes were here. She'd have to come back at some point.

She didn't.

Though by Friday of that week, she'd run so short of clothes—having worn the same two shirts and skirts the previous four days—she actually wore the sexy T-shirt to work.

Theo watched from afar. He'd worked out by now that she'd got what she wanted out of him—pregnancy—and that was that. She'd simply used the child's inheritance as an excuse to get away from him. And the fact that she looked pale and wan he put down to the beginnings of morning sickness. Although inside his chest he felt a pang whenever he saw her, he refused to acknowledge it as pity because feeling sorry for her would mean he cared.

And he didn't do emotional involvement!

But wearing the T-shirt to work was taking things too far. Most of the women on the team wore casual clothes to and from work as, during the day, their clothes were covered by a coloured coat, or their entire body was enveloped in green theatre pyjamas. But, still, he wasn't happy about her flaunting herself in the T-shirt—not happy at all—and he intended to tell her so. The majority of the team were off to Scoozi for dinner and an unofficial rundown of the past week, but when she didn't turn up there, he went to her flat, meeting Jean-Luc in the foyer.

'She's not home,' he said, and suspicion, like a shiny green serpent, coiled in Theo's belly.

'And you'd know where she is?' he asked, wondering if she was as close as being inside Jean-Luc's flat.

'Not a clue,' Jean-Luc said casually, 'but I knocked on her door a little earlier and got no answer.' He hesitated, then added, 'You two had a falling out?'

Theo scowled at him.

'It's none of your business,' he said.

Jean-Luc agreed, then added, 'I don't gossip but living in the flat beneath hers I couldn't help but notice that she's rarely home. She mentioned that you and she were…together. Nothing more, and I've said nothing to anyone although I have kept an eye on her place when she's not there. Am I right in assuming your affair is now over?'

'No!' Theo snapped, although he was beginning to wonder if it was.

But Jean-Luc took him at his word.

'Well, that's good because I'm sure everyone in the team has seen how much Grace has relaxed in the last few weeks. I know she tries to come across as tough and always on top of things, but I think that woman has a very soft, perhaps even vulnerable core.'

He walked out the front door, leaving Theo with no option but to follow. Jean-Luc turned left, away from the hospital, and Theo, not wanting to go home to an empty house that still smelt vaguely of orange blossom, turned right and trudged back to the hospital.

She *did* have a soft core.

She *was* very vulnerable.

He couldn't have been so wrong in his reading of her. Yet this action of walking away from him the moment she got pregnant made him wonder if he'd been totally taken in. The stand-off continued, although it was strange because when they'd been together they'd been forever running into each other at work, often stretching Theo's restraint to its limits, wanting to touch her as they nodded in passing, or discussed cases, pretending they were colleagues and nothing more.

But as the days went by he realised that they'd probably made opportunities to meet at work. That, or she was deliberately avoiding him now.

It made her heart ache just to see him. Grace had realised this the first week of their separation. She remembered telling Kelly that the heart didn't really feel emotion, but something in Grace's chest was aching almost constantly.

At night, lonely in her bed in the sterile, almost empty flat, she played their final conversation over and over in her head.

Was she wrong? Was she being pig-headed over the issue of him not telling her about the legacy? And did it really matter if her child ended up tremendously wealthy?

No, she guessed not. He or she could give away anything not needed. It was the not telling her—the deceit— the fact that Theo had a reason just as strong as she did for having a child, and he hadn't seen fit to tell her.

Not that any of this mattered. When it came down to the absolute basics, the more she was with Theo the more—she was about to say emotionally involved but alone in bed she could say the real word, love—she would grow to love him, so leaving him when she had to go home would be that much worse.

Work proved her solace and her release. She was remarkably well, perhaps feeling a little nausea in the early morning but the uneasiness disappeared once she'd eaten and walked briskly up the road to work. So, by the time she arrived in their section, she could concentrate on what had to be done.

She was going to work early these days, wanting to see the babies, especially Scarlett, before Theo was likely to be around. Alex's wife, Annie, had had her baby and Alex was on paternity leave, so Grace was in Theatre most days, working with Aldo and with Phil, having to use all her skills and showing them different techniques while she learnt new ones herself.

She nodded to Theo in passing, and if her heart raced when he was in Theatre with her, she was professional enough to focus all her attention on the operation, ignoring the little signals his body still transmitted to hers.

'We've got a heart!'

Becky poked her head into the theatre, yelling this news from the doorway. Grace was closing, the Norwood operation on a little boy nearing completion.

'It's up the north coast, a hospital at Murwillumbah. Who can go?'

Phil looked at the baby on the table, watched Grace put the final staple in his chest, then said, 'Would you go, Grace? I know you've done heart retrievals—it's your special field. I don't want to leave young Sam here and Aldo's on days off. Becky will arrange a team, an ambulance will take you to the airport—not the main airport but the one small planes use. From there, a volunteer will fly you up north. You'll have to do the operation then bring it back. Time wise…' he glanced up at the clock on the wall '…we'd expect you back by midnight and we'll have Scarlett all prepped and ready to go.'

Grace felt excitement leap in her body. A heart for Scarlett! What could be better?

'Of course I'll go. I leave now?'

Phil nodded.

'Becky will organise transport at the other end, and co-ordinate with the pilot. Whoever she finds to go as surgical assistant will have all the gear, and Theo's off-sider, Ryan Cooke, will do the perfusion and cardiople-gia.'

He hesitated then added, 'Good luck!'

There was a chorus of good-luck wishes from the team, as the little girl who had struggled so hard to stay alive had won all their hearts, but the voice she'd wanted to hear—Theo's deep-throated 'Good luck'—was absent.

Not that she had time to think of Theo. She stripped off her theatre gear and dragged on her clothes then hurried out to where Becky, Ryan and Jackie O'Connor, one of Alex's surgical assistants, were waiting, Jackie holding a medical case and cool box.

Grace took the time to check what was in the case—stitches and sutures, sterile gauze, retractor, sterile bags, lactate solutions—and in the cool box—ice.

'Our ambulance is downstairs—it'll be lights and sirens all the way so we'll have to hang on,' Ryan said.

'Another ambulance will meet you at the Gold Coast airport. The baby's being taken to Tweed Heads hospital and you'll operate there.' Becky took up the instructions. 'Their ambulance will take you back to the plane, the pilot will let us know when he's due to land in Sydney and we'll have transport waiting for you.'

Excitement built inside Grace, so much so that as the screaming vehicle sped through Sydney's streets she forgot about the man who hadn't wished her good luck and concentrated on what lay ahead.

The operation to remove a donor heart was delicate. It was important to keep a good length of vein and artery attached to the heart so it would be easier for Phil to attach them to Scarlett's vessels, and equally important to keep a reasonable length of the small vessels that came off the aorta and pulmonary artery to make attachment easier as well.

A man called Ron was waiting at the airfield and he led the three of them to a plane so small she marvelled that it could hold an engine strong enough to keep it up in the air, but Ron exuded confidence so she put her trust in him and as they flew north towards the border between New South Wales and Queensland, she rehearsed the operation in her head.

She had done similar operations before and knew she was more than competent to do it, but was it being pregnant that made her feel extra sorrow for the parents whose child had stopped breathing only twenty-four hours earlier?

And then there was the baby itself, doomed not to live. Rationally she knew that babies only died at birth or soon after because they had something radically wrong with them, but as the little plane flew through the dusk, the sinking sun far off in the west painting the sky orange and vermilion, she grieved for the baby as well.

'Storm building,' Ron said. He'd spoken little except to point out places she didn't know. He waved his hand towards the east where dark clouds roiled and rumbled.

'Will it worry us?' Jackie asked, and though Grace was still mentally rehearsing she caught Ron's part of the conversation.

'Might do later. I know you can't hurry things but I wouldn't stop for coffee if I were you,' he said, bringing the little plane into land on a brightly lit airfield.

'I don't drink coffee,' Grace assured him, feeling more at ease now they were on the ground.

Ron taxied towards some small buildings at one end of the runway and in the lights already lit around them she could see another ambulance waiting.

'That's your ride. He'll bring you back here. I'll be waiting.'

Grace thanked him and scrambled out of the plane behind Jackie, waiting for Ryan to emerge last before the three of them ran across the tarmac to the waiting ambulance. Ron hadn't sounded over-worried about the storm, but they'd better not dilly-dally just in case.

A woman who introduced herself but whose name went straight out of Grace's mind met them at the front door of the hospital and took them up to the operating theatre.

'Have you done retrievals before?' Grace asked Jackie.

'Quite a few,' the older woman replied.

'Then I'd like you to check the paperwork and make sure it's all in order. Things could be done differently here and we don't want to waste these people's wonderful gift because of a mix-up in the paperwork.'

Jackie nodded her understanding. She carefully read through all the official approvals, checked the necessary signatures were in place, then handed them to Grace for her signature.

The little baby was waiting for them in Theatre and Grace felt her own heart clamp tightly, as if someone had gripped it with a fist. She felt a surge of sympathy for the parents of the tiny child and blinked back emotion she never allowed herself to show at work.

Quietly, all of them touched by this lost life, they prepared—no theatre jokes tonight, no chat at all. Working carefully, she opened the chest and let the woman who'd met them know the heart was good— they would take it and use it. The woman would let Jimmie's know it was a go so they could start prepping Scarlett.

Then, making sure to take as much of the veins and arteries as possible, tying them off as she went, Grace gently removed the heart, passing it in her gloved hands to Ryan whose job it was to keep it in good condition until they got back to Sydney.

'You people get going, we'll close up.' A young surgeon who had been in Theatre with them made the offer.

Grace smiled at him.

'Thanks—but do it neatly, won't you?'

The young man nodded and as his eyes met hers she knew everyone in the room was as choked with emotion as she was. It didn't seem to matter how often you experienced death, the death of a baby always affected you. And this particular baby had given them a precious gift—the gift of life for Scarlett.

They rode back to the airfield in silence, meeting Ron who hurried them into the plane.

'Storm worsening between here and Sydney so buckle up tight, ladies and gent—we're in for a rough ride. Any of you feel queasy, there're sick bags under the seats.'

But rough didn't begin to describe it. As the little plane was tossed in the air like a leaf in a high wind, Grace clung to her seat and thought about her own unborn baby.

# CHAPTER EIGHT

'I'M GOING to see if I can get around it,' Ron said, turning the plane so they were now travelling inland instead of along the coast, 'and maybe beneath it, so don't panic if you feel us going down.'

'Whatever seems good to you,' Ryan assured him, then he started joking about whether any of their hearts would survive a crash and did they all have valid organ donor cards?

Medical humour, Grace knew, and Jackie was going along with it, while Ron concentrated grimly on keeping his tiny craft aloft.

Grace smiled but she wasn't listening to the talk, far more concerned about her own thoughts of immortality.

It wouldn't matter if she died tonight, because the baby would die with her, but later on—if anything ever happened to her—was it fair to leave a child without a parent?

Had she selfishly not thought of that?

Theo had asked if a child shouldn't have two parents and they'd talked around the subject a couple of times—

hypothetically, of course. She'd scoffed at the idea and had later pointed out that although it wasn't ideal, she'd grown up with one parent and done all right, but she'd had no choice in the matter. Of course a child needed two parents, especially if that was possible, if only for the security of knowing someone would always be there for them. Why hadn't she thought of this earlier?

Why hadn't she considered something happening to her, and the child being left an orphan?

Almost an orphan—it would still have a father!

But what could she do?

Explain her fears to Theo?

Ask him if he'd mind very much…not marrying her, of course, that would be asking too much of him, but being a little more involved than perhaps he'd first imagined he would, so the child would have the security of knowing him?

The plane dropped and Grace clung to the seat, noticing that Ryan's jokes had dried up and all four of them were now quiet—each absorbed in their own private thoughts.

Although hers were surely the most bizarre. She hadn't even asked Theo if he'd be content to be the child's guardian should something happen to her! How irresponsible was that?

And if he said no?

Could she marry someone else?

As if! She'd reached thirty-five years of age before meeting a man who made her hormones zing so how likely was it she'd meet another one in the near future— and one who'd want to bring up someone else's child?

Impossible!

'Are you OK?' Ryan asked, and she turned around
to find both him and Jackie looking anxiously at her.

'Yes, why?' she said, professional Grace back in
control—or almost.

'You were groaning,' Jackie told her.

'Thinking what a waste if we don't get the heart to
Sydney in time,' she lied, but she pushed her own
worries out of her head and concentrated on the plane,
wondering if positive thinking did indeed have power…

The team was in Theatre, Scarlett on the table, Phil
waiting only for the message from the co-ordinator of
the retrieval to say the plane had landed in Sydney
before he opened Scarlett's chest and began preparing
to put her on bypass.

Downstairs in the parents' room the Robinsons
would be sitting, probably holding each other, hope
sneaking into their hearts for the first time since
Scarlett's birth.

'I hate it when planes are late,' Phil said, then he gave
a sigh of relief as the theatre door opened and Becky
poked her head in.

'Are we set to go?' Phil said, but Becky shook her
head, then her voice, too, shook as she said, 'There's a
storm. The plane's gone off the radar.'

'What do you mean, the plane's gone off the radar?
How can a plane go off the radar?'

Theo hadn't realised he'd bellowed the questions
until everyone in the theatre turned to look at him, and
he read in the horror in all their eyes just how a plane
could go off the radar.

'The organ donor centre co-ordinator just phoned to

tell me that. There's a storm between the border and here and the air traffic control people think the pilot might just be avoiding that,' Becky said, but Theo could feel the icy dread that flooded through every member of the team in that room. People they knew—friends, even a lover—were on that plane.

*And* Scarlett's heart!

'They'll come through,' Phil said, apparently realising he had to take control before everyone's morale sank any further. 'Or land somewhere and wait out the blow.'

He touched Scarlett's cheek with a gloved finger.

'Only problem is time—how long they can keep the heart viable—but they'll do their best, little girl.'

Then he stepped away from the table.

'I think coffee and something to eat—half the team go now, the rest when that lot return. Silly to waste an opportunity to rest and eat when we might be up all night.'

He sounded cheerful and his suggestion made sense but no one moved towards a door.

Theo discovered that his main concern was that he didn't even know if Grace got travel sick—and whether being thrown around in a small plane in a storm would make her ill. And what about the baby?

She probably wouldn't allow herself such weakness, he decided, smiling wryly to himself, but the realisation of how little he knew of her bit deep.

And to think they'd fallen out over something so stupid! Did it really matter if the baby had money coming to him or her?

What mattered was that the baby was safe, because

now the plane-crash scenario had presented itself in full gory detail in his mind's eye, he realised he'd be devastated if anything were to happen to the baby's mother.

*Devastated?*

Surely not—that was an extreme reaction and that meant emotional involvement.

Which was when light dawned.

Of *course* he was emotionally involved with Grace! Get real here, use the word, he was in love. And not only *in* love, but he loved her—loved the little smile she gave when she was uncertain, loved the way her eyes went hazy when they made love, loved a little mole she had just above her left buttock…

He shook his head. Surely he couldn't be thinking of Grace's left buttock when her life was hanging in the balance—while she was in a tiny plane being flung around in the air, at the mercy of a storm.

The door opened and Becky, crying openly now, poked her head in.

'There's no news,' she said in a voice of such doom Theo wanted to shake her.

'Oh, come on now, everyone,' he said. 'Stop expecting the worst. The blokes that fly these planes are professionals—they know their job. The pilot will get them through so try some positive thinking here.'

Once again he must have spoken too loudly for the team members were all staring at him, as if the machine, not he, had spoken.

But Phil caught on.

'You're right. We're all here thinking gloom and doom. The pilot will get through—he's good—and little Scarlett's heart will arrive in time for us to use it. Now, I'm not suggesting people take a break, I'm ordering it. Go, the lot of you. Theo and I will stay here and we'll take a break when you get back.'

This time they did troop out, dropping off gloves and masks but going gowned into the little room where they could make tea or coffee and find a sandwich in the refrigerator or some biscuits in a tin.

'They don't look as if they're thinking positive thoughts, do they?' Phil remarked when he and Theo had the theatre to themselves.

'Not really,' Theo said, automatically responding to Phil's attempt at conversation while his mind was far away, praying that Grace would come through this—that he'd have the chance to talk to her, to explain…

'You've grown close, you and Grace.'

He stared at Phil. OK, so he'd told Grace people would guess they were having an affair but he'd also told her no one would mention it. Now here was Phil bringing up the subject.

'Yes,' Theo said, not wanting to say more, definitely not wanting to admit they'd fallen out nearly a fortnight ago and he was missing her like hell.

'So you're especially worried,' Phil persisted, and Theo shook his head.

'Oh, come on, Theo,' Phil said. 'For heaven's sake, man, you can talk to me about it. It was before you came here, but when Maggie and I first got together I nearly lost her through my own foolishness, and everyone in the unit knows something's happened between you and Grace in the last week or so. You can't both go around with silly smiles on your faces for ages then suddenly both look glum all the time without people putting two and two together.'

Theo knew he should protest the silly smiles part— Grace would never wear a silly smile—but he knew that wasn't the issue.

'Does she know you love her?'

Now Theo sighed. Phil was obviously going to pursue this subject. 'I didn't know myself till Becky said the plane was missing,' Theo admitted. 'It's the last thing I wanted or expected to happen but when I thought of her in danger, I knew.'

He considered the situation for a moment, then added, 'And I don't think she'd want to know anyway. It wasn't that kind of affair.'

'No?'

Phil spoke quietly, but before Theo could explain the situation—no emotional involvement on either side— Becky returned, this time with good news.

'They've found the plane. It went off course to escape the worst of the storm and should be in Sydney in another forty minutes.'

'Right!' Phil said. 'That gives everyone time to finish their break but go and tell them, Becky, I want them here ready to begin in thirty minutes. We'll go in the moment we hear they're on the ground. And send in a nurse from somewhere to keep an eye on Scarlett. Theo and I will take a break as well. It's going to be a long night.'

But although they did take a break the only thing Phil said regarding the personal conversation they'd had earlier was, 'I think you should tell her and let her decide what kind of an affair it was. And don't leave it until it's too late!'

She'd have to talk to him as soon as possible. That was the only decision Grace had arrived at by the time the little plane touched down in Sydney. Guilt that she'd been so irresponsible as to not think about the possibility of her own death nipped at her thoughts, but she'd have to set that aside—time enough for guilt once she'd spoken to Theo.

Scarlett was all ready to be put on pump when Grace walked into Theatre, a mask held across her mouth and nose, the cool-box in her hand.

'Give it to someone and scrub in, can you, Grace? I'll need you for the switch.'

One of the circulating nurses took the cool-box and Grace departed, but not before she'd looked across at Theo. She thought he was looking back at her, but in this theatre they all wore protective goggles over their eyes so it was hard to tell.

She scrubbed and came back in but this time when she looked at him she knew he must be looking back at her for he nodded.

Not that a nod meant much. It certainly didn't mean he was willing to be their baby's guardian.

Their baby…

If only…

'OK, Grace, take my place. I'd like you to detach Scarlett's heart and I'll get the new one ready to put in.'

Grace pulled on the magnifying loupe and headlight the assistant handed her and looked into Scarlett's small chest, seeing the tiny, misshapen heart she would have to remove. Someone—Phil or his assistant—had already cut away most of the ligaments that held the heart muscle in place and already inserted the tubes to connect her to the bypass machine.

She raised her head and looked at Theo.

'On pump,' she said, knowing this was one of the most pivotal moments of the operation. Had Theo got the pressure right? Would the machine successfully remove Scarlett's blood, re-oxygenate it, remove the carbon dioxide from it, and return it to her body in good time, and at a pressure her arteries could handle?

'On pump,' he repeated, telling her the machine was now doing the work. The heart lost colour almost immediately, and Aaron administered cardioplegia to stop it beating.

Grace worked around it, making sure there were no tiny blood vessels still connected, checking the coronary arteries were free of the muscle they supplied with blood, ready to start cutting and clamping them the moment the heart stopped.

Then the moment, one the whole team always seemed to feel—tense, as if the responsibility for stopping someone's heart rested on all their heads.

But Grace had no time for philosophy. She had to work, and work swiftly, for the shorter the time Scarlett was on pump the less chance there was of damage to some other part of her body.

Careful to leave little buttons of vessels for Phil to use when attaching the new heart, Grace removed the damaged, malformed heart and handed it to one of the theatre sisters, knowing it would go not into a bin, as

Kelly had suggested, but into another cool-box because someone, somewhere not too far away, would be studying genetic heart disease and every heart they had to inspect and dissect could provide new clues.

'OK, Grace, you've had a big day, you're now officially off duty, so beat it,' Phil told her, when he moved back into his position to attach the new heart.

'You don't need me?' she asked, knowing she couldn't go back to her soulless flat after such an emotional afternoon and evening.

'Definitely not. Go get some rest. You've been a trouper!'

Grace backed away reluctantly, glancing towards Theo whose entire attention was focussed on the machine.

She *had* to talk to him. She knew that, but as she stripped off her theatre clothes she realised he'd be in Theatre for at least another three hours and then if Scarlett left Theatre still on ECMO, which was highly likely, he'd want to stay with her for a while.

But as she showered, the aftermath of the tension of the flight draining the last of her energy from her body, she remembered she still had a key to his house. She'd go there and wait for him, because she *had* to talk to him, and if there was one thing her near-death experience in the plane had taught her, or at least reaffirmed, it was to not put off until tomorrow what could be done today.

OK, so he might not be home until tomorrow but at least she'd be there ready to talk.

She dressed again in the tired, dirty clothes she'd been wearing all day—with most of her clothes still at

Theo's she'd had no spares to leave at work—and made her way out of the hospital, knowing there'd be a cab outside—a cab to take her to Theo's house.

Theo watched her leave the theatre, his heart aching at the weariness he read in her movements, his joy in finding she was still alive tempered now by his concern for her.

He cursed the fact he couldn't leave with her—couldn't even speak to her or touch her.

Even think about her for more than a second, for his whole attention had to be on Scarlett and the machine. But later, as soon as he was free, he'd go to Grace, talk to her, tell her how he felt.

Phil worked with neat precision, making tiny stitches around the circumference of minute veins and arteries, putting a new heart into the chest of the little battler they'd all grown to love.

Love! As if anyone could cut love totally out of their life, for without it, what was life about?

And Grace—perhaps Grace could grow to love him, given time…

'OK,' Phil said, glancing up at Theo. 'Are we ready?'

It was the most climactic moment of a very tense operation and Theo could feel it in the air, everyone alert—praying…

'Off pump,' Phil said, and while his assistant and the surgical sisters peered into the chest cavity, seeking any signs of bleeding that would tell them a vein or artery connection had a leak, Phil and Theo watched the heart—watched the flaccid muscle slowly gaining form and colour as blood filtered back into it.

Would it beat?

Would they have to shock it?

Drugs were already running into Scarlett's blood, drugs to help the new heart beat, drugs to stop her immune system rejecting it. They'd done all they could...

The first movement was barely discernible then someone gave a cheer, and the little heart began to beat with a regular rhythm, so miraculous they all stood in awed silence and watched the movement.

'Check again for any haemorrhage,' Phil said, but although they'd made myriad small joins, there were no leaks. Now he had to stitch the pericardium back in place, then join the muscles and tendons they'd had to cut, ease back the lung and finally wire the sternum back together.

'Or will you leave it open?' someone asked, and Theo looked at Phil, wondering what he'd answer.

Babies' chests were sometimes left open after an operation when there was a chance something would fail and the surgeon might need to get back in there very quickly, but this time Phil shook his head.

'No,' he said, 'we'll close her up. This new heart's going to work, I can feel it in my bones.'

Another small cheer went up and the registrar began the task of closing, Phil stripping off his loupe and handing it to a circulating nurse before crossing the theatre to the bins and beginning to take off his theatre garb.

But before he left the theatre he looked back at Theo.

'I meant what I said,' he said, and Theo had to think

back—wondering exactly which bit of their conversation Phil now meant.

The bit about telling Grace?

Or about not leaving it too late?

He had to assume *that* was it, and as he watched over the baby girl through the remainder of her operation and went with her to Post-Op, wanting to be sure the ECMO machine was doing the least possible work, he considered it, deciding, when he finally walked out of the hospital in the pre-dawn light, that if he was going to tell her how he felt, he had to do it now!

He left his car in the hospital car park and walked down the road to Grace's flat, knowing the fresh air would make him feel more alive, although thinking about telling Grace he loved her had most of his nerves synapsing very efficiently.

The door into the foyer was locked, but as Theo walked around behind the big bush in the front yard, thinking he might find a stone and use the time-honoured method of throwing it against Grace's window, miracle of miracles, who should appear but Jean-Luc, opening the door and leaving it ajar, obviously just going out for a short time, a jog in the park from the look of the clothes he wore.

Theo didn't actually hide from the Frenchman, but he didn't make his presence known either, still feeling embarrassed about his last meeting at the house with Jean-Luc. And as Jean-Luc strode across the road, and stopped to stretch against the park fence, Theo slipped into the foyer and up the stairs to Grace's flat where he knocked quietly on the door, and then more loudly, finally realising she was either so fast asleep he'd never wake her with knocking, or she wasn't home.

But the only reason she'd not be home was because she was at the hospital—probably waiting with the Robinsons until Scarlett was out of Theatre. He should have thought of that, and checked there first, but right now he was too darned tired to go back up the road, too tired to even think, so he slid down onto the floor, rested his head against the doorjamb, and fell asleep.

Having convinced herself Theo wouldn't mind if she just rested on his bed while she waited for him, Grace lay down and was soon fast asleep.

She slept well and deeply, the various tensions of the day draining out of her, the smell of Theo on the pillows and the sheets so comforting that as she turned over and hazily came part-awake, she wondered if she could stay snuggled in Theo's bed for ever.

But waking, well into the morning, and finding him still not home sent her into a panic. What had she been thinking, coming here like this?

They had not been together for weeks—wasn't it feasible he already had another woman in his life?

And what if he came home with her? How much trouble would he be in if his current girlfriend found Grace in his bed?

But the thought of Theo with another woman made her weepy, so she decided she wouldn't think about that again. She'd have a shower, put on clean clothes—at last—pack up the things she'd left here, and go quietly back home. Yes, she had to talk to Theo, but she'd been emotionally overwrought when she'd decided she had to do it right there and then.

Coming to his house like this!

How could she?

He saw a cab turning out of his street but cabs were always around in this area. It wasn't until he opened his front door and smelt Grace's perfume that he wondered about the cab because she had definitely been there. Not only been there, but she'd packed up all her things.

She was gone!

He'd left it too late.

Or had he?

If she was in the cab he'd seen she'd be home in a few minutes, but in the meantime she'd have her mobile on.

He tried it, only to find it was turned off.

He made a cup of coffee for himself then phoned the flat, but no joy there.

His neck ached from the awkward position in which he'd fallen asleep and his exhaustion was so great he knew he had to sleep. He tipped the coffee down the sink, rinsed the cup, then made his way up to his bedroom where Grace's perfume was even stronger.

It pulled him towards the bed, and, wrapping his arms around a pillow that still, miraculously, smelt of her, he went to sleep.

# CHAPTER NINE

GRACE directed the cab to her home address first so she could drop off her small suitcase, then, as anxious as a relative, she headed back to the hospital to see how Scarlett was doing.

'She's so well I don't think she'll be with us much longer,' Jasmine told Grace, taking her to the crib where the little girl lay, flanked by her parents. 'She'll be graduating to the ward within days, won't she, Mrs Robinson?'

Mrs Robinson's smile was enough to ease a lot of the pain in Grace's heart, and as she looked at the little girl for whom she'd been through so much, she knew every second of the tortuous flight had been worthwhile.

Worthwhile too, in other ways, she knew that. So she'd overreacted, rushing off to Theo's the way she had last night, but she had to talk to him. If he didn't want to be the baby's guardian—didn't want more than the rights she'd originally proposed—then she'd have to live with that.

And with heartache as well, because hearts—can you hear me, Kelly?—definitely did ache.

She left the hospital, this time not walking back towards her flat but down the other road, to the brasserie—a place that had somehow become 'their' place. Although only lovers—as in people in love—had special places...

Sitting over chai and fruit toast in the pretty courtyard, deserted now the 'breakfast before work' clientele had departed, Grace thought back to when she and Theo had first sat here and she'd put her proposition to him. She should have realised then how very kind he was, not mocking her, as many men would have done, or suggesting they leap straight into bed.

No, he'd treated her halting explanations seriously, had even seemed to understand how she'd come to the stage where she was asking a virtual stranger to help her conceive a baby.

But, then, he'd been through such terrible trauma himself—of course he'd be empathic. And he'd been gentle too—kind...

'I've been searching the city for you!' The kind and gentle man sounded extremely angry. 'Worrying about you. And I've got a crick in my neck from sleeping outside your front door.'

Grace stared at him, wondering if he was a mirage her thoughts had conjured up.

No, her thoughts had been conjuring up a very different Theo, not this shadow-eyed, drawn-faced streak of angry masculinity standing over her.

'You slept outside my door? Why would you do that?'

His shoulders relaxed and he slumped into a chair.

'Oh, Grace, if there's one thing a person can expect

from you it's to expect the unexpected. Not why am I angry but why did I sleep outside your door? Because I wanted to talk to you, of course.'

'Oh!' she whispered, and held her hand against her lips, not wanting anything more to come out before she'd thought about it. Not that the hand over her lips routine worked. Oh, no, here she was, blurting out the first thing that came into her head.

'I went to your place. I wanted to talk to you as well. I had a key. I hope you didn't mind that I used it and went in, then I fell asleep…'

'You were in my house and you fell asleep?' He stood up again as if he needed more space to contain his anger, although she wasn't entirely sure the emotion simmering in his tense body was all anger. 'I'm running all over town looking for you and you're sleeping in my bed?'

'I didn't mean to sleep but I was tired.'

Fortunately at that stage a waitress appeared to ask Theo if he wanted anything. Grace took advantage of the interruption to take a deep breath, settle the nerves that were doing little dances of excitement because Theo had wanted to talk to her, and decide to take charge of the situation before it became even more farcical.

'Sit down, Theo,' she ordered when the waitress had taken his order and disappeared towards the kitchen. 'I'm sorry if you were inconvenienced, *and* about the crick in your neck but I *do* want to talk to you and here's a good place to do it.'

He sat, but obviously wasn't mollified.

'Why?' he asked.

'Why talk?'

'No, why here?'

She had to smile.

Then take another deep breath.

'Because if we were at your place or at my place we'd get very little talking done.' She smiled again. 'You know that.'

The darkness in his eyes she'd taken for anger now faded and a glimmer she knew well took its place, but he nodded his agreement.

'So talk,' he added, in case his nod wasn't enough.

Easy for him to say!

Third deep breath. She had to stop this—she'd pass out.

'On the plane,' she began, but before she could continue Theo broke in.

'You should never have been on that plane. You should have told Phil you were pregnant and couldn't go. You've got two lives to think about now. It was madness.'

She stared at him, unable to believe this was the, oh, so professional Theo Corones talking.

'Theo, it's my job, I had to go, pregnant or not, and I'll continue to do my job wherever it takes me. And this is my talking time, not yours. As I was saying, on the plane, when it flew into a bit of trouble—'

'Bit of trouble? You were off the radar, Grace! It was assumed you'd crashed!'

'Theo?'

He stopped talking, staring off into the corner of the courtyard, but she saw how drawn and tired he looked and suddenly regretted starting the conversation now.

'I'm sorry, you've been up all night, and worrying, too, over Scarlett. We'll sit here while you have your breakfast and we'll talk some other time.'

He spun around and though he sounded angry it wasn't anger she could see in his eyes. It was something else.

'Talk some other time? That's just the problem. That's what I realised last night—there might not be another time.'

And because his thinking was so in tune with hers she reached across the table and took his hand.

'Oh, Theo, that's exactly what I thought on the plane. I realised how selfish I'd been, how unfair to the baby. I started to worry about who would bring up our child— well, not so much bring up but protect our child if something happened to me. You asked me once before about the ethical considerations of bringing up a child with only one parent and I scoffed at you, but you were right. Who will be the child's security if that one parent goes? Oh, I have my father, and friends who have children and no doubt when I'd thought it through I'd have made provisions for guardianship but, Theo, I know it's a lot to ask, particularly as you never wanted a child and especially as you don't want emotional attachment to it, and I'm sorry I got upset because of the financial stuff, but I thought if you're going to be keeping in touch because of the child's future responsibilities I wondered if perhaps you could be around a little bit more and he or she could really get to know you so—'

'Stop right there!'

He removed his hand from hers so he could hold it up, like a traffic policeman at a breathalyser station.

'Have you actually heard yourself? Have you heard the drivel you're spouting? Friends who could be guardians? *I'm* the child's father—guardianship isn't something you decide. This is *my* child you're talking about.'

'But you didn't want involvement,' Grace reminded him. 'It's the one thing you didn't want and, knowing what you've been through, I can understand that.'

Theo stared across the table at the beautiful woman who had wreaked such havoc in his life. She had no idea—not a clue—how things had changed between them.

Or had things changed?

Was it only him feeling all the things he'd never wanted to feel again? The love he felt for Grace was a first—a very different love to the attraction-convenience kind of love he'd shared with Lena. But that wasn't the issue—what was at stake was Grace. And would she be prattling on the way she was if she felt anything at all for him?

The way she spoke, she certainly wasn't seeing them as a couple...

'Well?' she demanded, and he realised he didn't have a clue how to go on.

Make a fool of himself by declaring his love?

Not only make a fool of himself, but embarrass her at the same time?

'I think I should go back and sleep outside your door. I might have got a crick in my neck but I wasn't so confused,' he muttered, as the waitress appeared with his order. He looked at the fabled Big Breakfast the brasserie served and knew he should be hungry but all of a sudden bacon and eggs and sausages and tomatoes and hash browns had no appeal at all.

What he wanted was Grace.

In his life, in his bed, sharing a breakfast table with him for ever.

And all *she* wanted was a promise that he'd take care of her child if something happened to her...

'I think I'll go now,' he said, standing up and pushing back his chair with his legs. 'Maybe we'll both make more sense when we've had some sleep.'

'You haven't said anything to make sense or not,' Grace pointed out, in her usual practical, precise way. 'And I've had some sleep. But if you need to sleep before you decide if you want to be a guardian to your own child then that's fine by me!'

Theo peered down at her.

She sounded huffy, and huffy wasn't a word he'd ever associated with Grace, but maybe he was just so tired he was misreading her.

But just in case he wasn't, he'd better check it out.

'Are you OK?' he asked.

She glared at him—definitely huffy.

'Of course I'm not all right. I nearly died last night, Theo, and it made me think about my life and the life of my child, and when I try to explain it to someone who I think just might care, what do I get? You asserting you'll choose a guardian, which is all very well for you, but what if I don't agree?'

Grace stopped and shook her head.

'Actually,' she said, 'that isn't what I wanted to discuss with you at all. This conversation has got so far off track it's ridiculous. I probably started at the wrong place and now I can see you're exhausted so we won't say any more now, but do eat your breakfast. You'll sleep better if you've eaten. And if you want company, I'll sit here and not talk at all.'

He studied her for a moment, then he sat—he *was* hungry. And maybe sitting a while with Grace would calm him down, bring back the balm to his soul that he'd felt when she'd been living with him.

He cut the sausages, pushed a small piece on his fork, added a snippet of egg and began to eat, realising when he was halfway through that Grace could well be hungry too.

'They're not as tasty as your South African sausages,' he said, cutting another piece and pushing it onto his fork, 'but they're very good. Try it?'

He offered the fork across the table to her and as she leaned forward, lips opening, to slide it into her mouth, he remembered Phil saying not to leave it too late.

'I love you,' he said, then wondered if the Heimlich manoeuvre really worked as Grace began to choke on the sausage.

'You what?' she demanded, when, flushed and breathless, she rested back in her chair.

'I love you,' he repeated, the words sounding better the second time—firmer, more positive, no longer tentative and hesitant. 'I realised it last night when we thought the plane had crashed. I realised I loved you and I'd never had a chance to tell you. Never had a chance to say how beautiful you are, not only outside but inside as well, and how caring and considerate, for all you hide it under your cool, competent manner. And how you're never quite sure when you're being teased because you're such a down-the-line person and haven't had a lot of teasing. And I love that little hitch you get in your breathing when your uncertainty comes through and I want to kill the rat who left you at the altar and never told you what a wonderful, sexy woman you are.'

She stared at him, pale now, then she smiled.

'All this over sausages and eggs for breakfast,' she said. 'Should we have been having cooked breakfasts earlier?'

He shook his head, relieved now he'd said what needed to be said, but very uncertain about its reception. She was teasing *him* now, wasn't she?

He hoped she was but he didn't have a clue, although she did reach across the table and take his hands, which had abandoned his cutlery and already pushed the remainder of his breakfast to one side.

'You didn't want this, Theo. You didn't want emotional involvement.'

She looked very serious—worried even—but that was Grace, already blaming herself for him falling in love with her, worried because he'd been so adamant he didn't want to fall in love again.

'That was before I met you,' he told her, searching for the right words to say to this woman who'd been hurt before, so badly it was hard for her to believe—to trust.

'And before I realised that life without emotional involvement—without love—is nothing more than a half-life—a kind of going-through-the-motions pretence at living. For years I've been telling myself it's enough—the satisfaction I get in my job, the pleasure in seeing my house take shape—and by the way, I've rendered my oven and it's ready to try. But even that failed to delight me because you weren't there and I couldn't turn to you and watch as you admired it.'

'You finished it?'

Grace knew this wasn't the issue here but all this other stuff—Theo loved her? Well, it was just too much to take in, let alone consider, although the warm, soft, rosy feeling inside of her suggested it was OK.

'Grace!' he said, so firmly she knew she *had* to answer him—not about the oven but about love.

And love was something that she knew very little about.

Something that made her scared—no, terrified…

'That's good,' she began, feeling her way into this extraordinary conversation. 'Because it kind of fits with what I really wanted to say when I started waffling on earlier. You see—'

She thought she was doing quite well but Theo had retrieved his hands and was standing up again.

'Come on,' he said, not brusquely but it was definitely an order. 'We're going home.'

'Home?' she echoed, definitely bleating now.

'Home to my place, home to bed. You're right, I need to sleep and I won't sleep if you're not in bed beside me so you're coming too, and somehow we'll get all this sorted out.'

All what? she wanted to ask, but in truth she rather fancied Theo in this masterful mood and her body missed his so much she was aching for him, and if he loved her, surely he'd love the baby, so that would work out all right in the end…

She followed him out of the brasserie, walked with him up the street to the hospital, even allowed him to do up her seat belt without protest, then as he drove—still masterful—towards his house, she felt herself relaxing because it seemed so right, somehow, to be driving home with Theo.

Which was when she realised that home would always be where Theo was…

What was she *thinking*?

Yes, she'd thought in terms of them spending time together once the baby was born—perhaps holidays—definitely visiting back and forth, but never, for all that her love for Theo had grown and blossomed inside her from the first time they'd made love, had she considered a permanent situation between them.

Because she'd been so sure he didn't love her.

And she'd been committed to honouring his determination to not be emotionally involved.

But if he loved her…

Joy fluttered in her heart and she hoped that some time she might meet up with Kelly again because hearts could feel joy as well as sadness, and love and all the other emotions. Her liver wasn't doing anything, thank you very much.

'What are you thinking about?' Theo asked as he parked outside his house.

'About livers!'

The words came out before Grace had time to stop them, but it didn't matter, for Theo was laughing, a sound so joyous her heart began to dance and also, she rather thought, hum a few happy bars of music.

'Oh, Grace, do you wonder I fell in love with you?' he said. 'You come out with the most unexpected things. You are full of surprising moments of joy—and an endless source of delight, not all of which, my beautiful Grace, is physical.'

And with that he leaned across, wrapped his arms around her and kissed her thoroughly. So thoroughly, in fact, they were both a little shaky and definitely dishevelled as they clambered out of the car and hurried into his house.

No words were spoken—the time for words was past—as they hurried up the stairs, stripping off clothes as they went, discarding them carelessly so by the time they fell into bed they were naked.

But here the tempo changed, Grace feeling confirmation of Theo's words of love in every touch, and touch he did, his hands exploring her as if this was their very first time together.

Or was he relearning her as she was now relearning him, revelling in the satin smoothness of his skin, in the hardness of the muscles beneath it, in the masculine weight of his arms and the insistent teasing of his fingers? And as they joined he said the words again. 'I love you, Grace.' A declaration, her name, a little later, a shout of joy as well as of possession.

But for herself?

As she returned to earth from the far-flung place his loving transported her, she had to think about things.

Oh, she loved him, and had for some time, but telling him, that was different. How could she say it when love had once before been thrown back in her face? When someone she'd thought returned her love had made a mockery of it, and, through her love, of her?

She snuggled deeper into Theo's sheltering arms, at

peace yet not entirely, but he was sleeping now and talk could wait, for now she was content just to be…

Not a word! Not even when her gasp and shattered cry of release had told him she'd reached orgasm. And now, when he'd awoken, he found her curled against him, sleeping peacefully, and he knew no more of how she felt than he had earlier.

Or, in fact, during their entire relationship.

Which just might, he admitted to himself with a sigh, be because he'd been so adamant about not wanting emotional involvement.

How stupid had *that* been?

He eased out of the bed, careful not to wake her, pulled on some briefs and went downstairs, sorry he'd finished the oven in the lonely days and nights when he'd been missing Grace. He made a cup of coffee and took it into the courtyard, sitting down with his back against the sun-warmed brick wall. But he didn't find the peace he craved because in five short weeks she'd left her mark here as well, and he could see her snipping wayward shoots off his espaliered apple, hear her laughing over some little incident at work as he cooked their dinner.

But all she'd wanted was a baby—he'd known that from the start.

'That coffee smells good. Good morning, or is it good afternoon?'

She was wearing one of his shirts that barely covered her butt and made her glorious legs look so good he wanted to tell her she should wear less more often.

Then not tell her, because he would hate for another man to see her as she was now.

'I'm in a clothes bind again,' she said, for all the world as if nothing had happened between them and they were back where they'd been before he'd brought up the child as his father's heir. 'All my gear is back at my place and somehow…' she blushed in the way he found irresistible '…I tore the skirt I was wearing when we came in.'

He sipped his coffee and wondered just how long this nothing conversation would go on, then he suddenly realised that this was Grace being Grace again—cool, competent, classy, and covering up such a welter of insecurities he didn't know how she did it.

But although he'd seen through the act, he wasn't going to let on—not just yet. After all, hadn't she been keeping him waiting?

'Coffee?' he offered, and that's when she snapped.

'Of course I don't want coffee. We were supposed to be talking, to be sorting things out, and suddenly we're back in bed together and nothing's sorted—'

He knew that now she'd started she'd keep going for it was how she got uncomfortable things said, so he broke in.

'Except me telling you I love you—surely that's a step in the right direction.'

Her hands stole to her cheeks, scarlet again.

'I thought I might have dreamt that part,' she said, so hesitant he had to stand up and put his arms around her.

'You didn't dream it. I do love you, and while it might make things complicated for you, you'd better learn to live with it because I'm going to love you for a long, long time, Grace Sutherland. And loving you I want to live with you, with you and our child and whatever other children we might have. I said before I'd like to see South Africa—moving there is no problem to me.'

She was looking at him, her eyes still wary, as if afraid to accept what he was saying, while Theo himself was growing increasingly anxious because, although his declaration was going quite well, there didn't seem to be any answering declaration from the woman to whom he was professing such love.

For one panicky moment he wondered if he'd got it wrong—totally wrong—and she didn't love him, but he'd learned to read her and he thought...

Now her clear blue eyes met his.

'It was living together I wanted to talk about,' she said, so quietly he had to strain, and hold her closer, in order to hear the words. 'On the plane. That's what I was thinking, that it would be best for the baby, but I knew how you felt and didn't know how to ask you if you'd mind, and also it seemed to me as if I was going back on our agreement even to think about it, but, Theo, if you love me...'

He kissed her gently on the lips.

'I do love you and although it's hard for you to believe that, you've got to try, maybe say it to yourself a hundred times a day. "Theo loves me." Three little words—not hard.'

Could she hear his tension in the huskiness of his voice that she said the words then returned his kiss, pressing her lips against his before saying them again?

'Maybe a million times a day,' she said, a radiant smile breaking out on her face.

'Just as long as you believe it,' he growled, and held her tight against his body, delighting in the feel of Grace in his arms again, considering going back to bed, refusing to think about the fact she might not love him…

He deepened the kiss, ruthlessly dragging such a response from her that she trembled against him, whispering his name in breathless gasps.

'Bed?' she suggested, but he shook his head.

'No way,' he said, and held her aroused body a little away from him so he could look into her flushed face and starry eyes. 'Not until we've talked, and I don't mean about arrangements and agreements and babies having two parents. I want other talk—it's time for love talk, Grace.'

The colour faded from her cheeks and once again he was gripped by a fear that he'd got it wrong, but her chin tilted upward and her eyes met his.

'I've only told one other man I loved him, Theo,' she said quietly, 'and he destroyed that love in the most public and painful way possible. I promised myself I'd never fall in love again, but almost from the moment we met I found myself being drawn to you—not only with our atoms hooking, but our minds as well. You were kind, and considerate and understanding, and suddenly there you were in my heart. Although I'd told young Kelly that love didn't live in hearts, I knew you'd taken up residence in mine. But knowing how you felt, I didn't want to embarrass you by telling you.'

Theo hugged her close again.

'If I promise not to be embarrassed, will you tell me now?' he murmured against the soft gold hair that smelled of orange blossom.

She nodded then eased away from him.

'I love you, Theo, with all my heart and all whatever other organs might be involved with love.'

'Thank heavens for that!' he said, giving her a hug of absolute joy. '*Now* we can go back to bed!'

# CHAPTER TEN

SCARLETT was doing well with her new heart—so well, in fact, they were considering moving her out of the PICU. Grace stood looking down at the little baby, thinking of her own child—hers and Theo's—growing inside her, when Mrs Robinson appeared.

'I know they're not supposed to tell, the social welfare people, but my husband had to know who'd arranged the money so we could come down and be with Scarlett and now we want to thank you,' she said quietly, handing Grace a bulky parcel.

'Oh, no, I don't want a gift—my gift was the pleasure of being able to help,' she said, but Mrs Robinson insisted she have it so Grace unwrapped it and there, folded carefully, lay the most beautiful, delicately knitted, cream shawl.

'It's from wool from our own sheep—super fine—and my mother spun it then I knitted it. I've knitted one for each of the children so they'd each have one to pass on to their children, and at first we thought Scarlett was going to be a twin so this time I knitted two, but now I'd like you to have it for your baby.'

'My baby?' Grace queried, unable to believe this was happening—first that Mrs Robinson had found out about her gift, and now that the woman knew she was expecting.

'I told you my mother was the seventh daughter of a seventh daughter—she said Scarlett would be saved by a pregnant woman and looking at you, seeing your smile when you look at Scarlett and all the babies here, it's just confirmed what Mum said. You *are* pregnant, aren't you?'

Grace nodded, but had no idea what to say. She could feel heat rising in her cheeks, and knew if she tried to talk she'd probably cry, but fortunately, as she held the beautiful shawl in her hands, Theo came in and apparently took in the situation with one glance.

'Ah, first baby gift, and what a beautiful one,' he said, picking up the shawl and holding it out so Grace could see the lacy, intricately knitted pattern. 'Thank you, Mrs Robinson, we'll treasure this.'

Mrs Robinson beamed with pride, and Grace, though exceptionally grateful for Theo's intervention, was now even more confused.

'How did you know what it was?' she demanded a little later when they found themselves alone in the tearoom.

He laughed and kissed her lightly on the lips.

'One look at your face was enough to tell me. You were shocked and delighted and happy and bamboozled all at once and I thought, There's my beautiful Grace, all uncertain again because someone's done something nice for her and she doesn't know how to handle it.'

He kissed her again.

'You have to believe in yourself, Grace Sutherland. Oh, you do as far as your profession goes—you know you're good at what you do—but in your personal life you have to accept that you are one of the world's nicest, kindest, most caring and concerned people, and you don't have to hide that niceness and kindness and caring and concern behind a screen of polite disinterest, or brusqueness, or a distant manner because no one's ever going to take you for granted again. If they do, they'll have me to answer to and I can be a very formidable man when I like!'

He sounded so fierce Grace had to laugh, and, laughing, she fell into his arms, so when Phil wandered in he found them locked together, not laughing now but reaffirming all the words they'd spoken over the last few days with a kiss.

'Got things sorted, then,' Phil said, walking past them to put on the kettle.

'You might say that,' Theo told him, then, because it was only Phil, he went on kissing Grace.

MILLS & BOON

# MEDICAL™
## On sale 6th March 2009

### THE CHILDREN'S DOCTOR'S SPECIAL PROPOSAL
*by Kate Hardy*

Rhys Morgan's charms are legendary, but Katrina, bruised from a previous relationship, assumes she's below her new boss's radar. When their shared commitment to their patients turns to passion, Rhys wonders whether Katrina could make him believe in happy ever after...

### ENGLISH DOCTOR, ITALIAN BRIDE
*by Carol Marinelli*

Consultant Hugh Armstrong has returned to Australia, unable to forget the woman he left behind – Bonny Azetti – all those years ago. Now he is Bonny's boss and she seems more out of bounds than ever but their passion continues to grow...

### THE DOCTOR'S BABY BOMBSHELL
*by Jennifer Taylor*

Gorgeous doctor Ben Nicholls has never forgotten the day Dr Zoë Frost walked away from him. Two years later, Zoë reappears and they find their attraction is as strong as ever... Amidst this new-found happiness, how can Zoë face Ben and tell him her secret – she is pregnant with his baby!

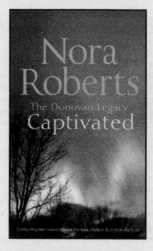

# Passion. Power. Suspense.
# It's time to fall under the spell
# of Nora Roberts.

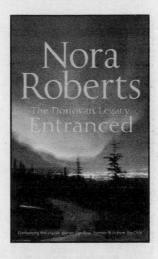

A missing child. A desperate mother.
A private investigator running out of time.

Reluctantly, Mel Sutherland had to accept Sebastian
Donovan's aid. She was cynical about his powers
and suspicious of his motives. But as the clock ticked,
Sebastian unfailingly knew how to follow the
abductor's tracks and Mel had to make up her mind.
Was Sebastian's gift real? Or was something far
more sinister at work?

**This is the second volume in Nora Roberts'
spellbinding *The Donovan Legacy*.**

## Available 6th February 2009

# Passion. Power. Suspense.
# It's time to fall under the spell
# of Nora Roberts.

When Boone Sawyer came into her life,
Anastasia Donovan had to protect herself
and her magic at all costs.

Then she was confronted with a terrifying
threat. With a child's future at stake,
Anastasia could not deny her powers,
even if it meant risking her own life.

**This is the third volume in Nora Roberts'
spellbinding *The Donovan Legacy*.**

## Available 6th March 2009

# The Wedding Planners

Join these three beautiful brides-to-be as all their wedding dreams come true!

Available
16th January 2009

These three lucky ladies have a millionaire's ring on their finger!

Available
20th February 2009

Planning perfect weddings...
finding happy endings!

# FREE

## 4 BOOKS AND A SURPRISE GIFT!

We would like to take this opportunity to thank you for reading this Mills & Boon® book by offering you the chance to take FOUR more specially selected titles from the Medical™ series absolutely FREE! We're also making this offer to introduce you to the benefits of the Mills & Boon® Book Club™—

- ★ **FREE home delivery**
- ★ **FREE gifts and competitions**
- ★ **FREE monthly Newsletter**
- ★ **Books available before they're in the shops**
- ★ **Exclusive Mills & Boon Book Club offers**

Accepting these FREE books and gift places you under no obligation to buy; you may cancel at any time, even after receiving your free shipment. Simply complete your details below and return the entire page to the address below. You don't even need a stamp!

**YES!** Please send me 4 free Medical books and a surprise gift. I understand that unless you hear from me, I will receive 6 superb new titles every month for just £2.99 each, postage and packing free. I am under no obligation to purchase any books and may cancel my subscription at any time. The free books and gift will be mine to keep in any case.

M9ZEE

Ms/Mrs/Miss/Mr.........................................Initials ........................................
**BLOCK CAPITALS PLEASE**

Surname .........................................................................................................

Address ..........................................................................................................

..........................................................................................................................

.........................................................Postcode .........................................

Send this whole page to:
The Mills & Boon Book Club, FREEPOST CN81, Croydon, CR9 3WZ